BUCKY
GETS
BUSTED

The Bucky Stone Series

BUCKY
GETS
BUSTED

David B. Smith

REVIEW AND HERALD® PUBLISHING ASSOCIATION
HAGERSTOWN, MD 21740

Copyright © 1994 by
Review and Herald® Publishing Association

The author assumes full responsibility for the accuracy of all facts and
quotations as cited in this book.

This book was
Edited by Gerald Wheeler
Designed by Bill Kirstein
Cover art by Scott Snow
Typeset: 11/13 Optima

PRINTED IN U.S.A.

99 98 97 96 95 94   10 9 8 7 6 5 4 3 2 1

R&H Cataloging Service
Smith, David B   1955-
    Bucky gets busted.

    I. Title.

          813.54

ISBN 0-8280-0807-8

CHAPTER 1

A BAD VARSITY SCHEDULE

The chlorinated water of the community pool still had a trace of chill to it as an unexpected spray landed on Bucky. "Hey!" He raised up in mock protest at the little boy who had accidentally created the splash.

"Lighten up." Dan laughed as he moved his towel away from the damp spot. "Man, that sun feels good."

The warm March weather seemed to melt away the tensions of the just-completed basketball season as the two enjoyed a leisurely Sunday afternoon. Several high school girls eyed the young men as they trooped past on their way to the snack bar.

"You seen anything of Deirdre this weekend?"

Dan shook his head with a frown. "Well, I guess we're broken up. Kind of."

"What do you mean, 'kind of'?"

The stocky youth shrugged. "I dunno. We talked some about, you know, church and stuff. And she said, 'Well, I sure heard all of *that* before.' So I kind of dropped it."

Bucky shifted his towel to take advantage of the shifting shade patterns next to the huge pool. "That's tough, man. She's . . ." His voice trailed off as he remembered back to their sophomore year and his own special moments with the ice-blond girl. Despite the difficulty in dating a girl who had vehemently announced her disinterest in Christianity, Deirdre was "one heart-stopping babe," as both of them knew.

Standing, Dan stretched with a groan. "Gonna go in again?"

"Nah. I'm all warm now."

His friend scanned the girls around the pool. "Yeah, guess I'll call it a day too." He motioned toward the locker room. "Come on, let's get out of here."

Out in the parking lot they paused by Dan's blue sports car. "Baseball next week," the older boy reminded.

"Yeah." Bucky grinned. Despite the painful ending to the season two years ago and last year's broken arm, even the mention of baseball always brought a shiver of excitement. "I know you're sick of hearing it—but do you think we got a shot at varsity?"

Dan laughed. "Man, Stone, you're always thinkin' about the big time!"

"Well, do we?"

A shrug. "I don't know. Two years in a row we've

cheesed it. Brayshaw's gettin' desperate to win *something* in baseball." He looked directly at his friend. " 'Course, last year you didn't even play. That ain't gonna help when it comes time to make up the varsity roster."

Bucky nodded. "Yeah, you're right." He reached in his pocket for the keys to his white Toyota. "We'll see what happens."

"OK. See you." Dan rumbled his way out of the parking lot, squealing his tires as usual.

Monday at school marked a switch in Bucky's chemistry lab assignment as he adjusted his schedule for the final quarter. "At least juniors get first pick," he muttered to himself as he made his way into the large science building and found his table.

Already two other students were setting up the afternoon project. "You Stone?" The boy, a stocky student with reddish-brown hair, wore a protective apron with a huge rip in the front. A big green Oakland A's logo poked its way through the tear.

"Yeah." Bucky pulled on a second apron and tied it behind him. "What are we working on?"

"Aaaah, the usual exciting stuff." The boy nodded to the girl standing next to him. "Tracy, here, has the experiment slip."

Bucky had to smile in spite of himself as he glanced at the girl. She looked to be all of four foot eleven and had the reddest hair he'd ever seen.

She looked up at him. "What's so funny?"

He gulped. "Nothing. I guess I . . ."

The other boy snickered. "He's just staring because he ain't never seen a fourth-grader trying to pass herself off as a junior in high school."

"Ha ha." She gave him a withering look. "You're so smart, Jonathan, why don't you tally up my results and do all the math for us?"

Jonathan reached over and patted the girl on the head. "Don't mind her," he advised Bucky. "Just because she's doing an honors project for the state competition, she thinks she can boss ordinary boys like us around. We'll be lucky if she lets us hold her spare calculator batteries for her."

As the afternoon session proceeded, Bucky had to acknowledge that Jonathan was at least half right. Tracy was smart! All during the experiment she kept up a steady stream of scientific observations that weren't even in the chem manual. It was the kind of mental display a guy would shrug off if it weren't for the little witticisms that punctuated every other sentence. At the conclusion of the project she wrote up the findings, along with two alternate interpretations that neither boy had noticed. Her handwriting had a precise femininity to it, but she signed off at the bottom with a flourish.

"So, are you going to play ball this spring?" Tracy peeled off her white apron and stacked up a formidable pile of books. She gave him a mischievous look.

"I, uh . . ." Bucky still felt unnerved by the redhead's intellect and personality. "Yeah, I guess."

"Jonathan and I'll come out and watch you sometime." She gave her bubbly little laugh. "See if your batting average is a little better than your GPA."

"Hey, who said I didn't have a decent GPA?" Bucky pretended to scowl.

Jonathan draped an arm around him. "Face it, pal, no matter what it is, it's a ways down the ladder from Miss Genius here." He pretended to sniff at Tracy. "It doesn't take a laptop computer to figure out her 4.0."

"Are you kidding? A four point?"

Tracy shrugged. "So far."

Bucky drove over to the bank still thinking about the exchange. Ever since beginning school at Hampton Beach High, good grades had come easily for him. But he had to admit that Tracy's 4.0 had rattled him.

The two-hour shift at First California Bank went smoothly. Careful to read all the employee update bulletins, Bucky rarely found himself stymied by a new banking procedure. Twice during the afternoon session he pointed out mistakes to the new girl training at window 4.

It was just starting to get dark when he went out to the parking lot. To his surprise Dan was waiting for him. "What's up, my man?"

Dan pulled out a tattered sheet of paper. "Check this out."

The younger student squinted to make it out. "What is it?"

"Baseball schedule." Dan kicked at a rock. "Varsity and JV. Look at it."

"Man, it's got a bunch of Friday nights on it."

"Tell me about it." Dan growled out the last words. "Five for varsity and four for JV."

Bucky felt the light optimism of the afternoon begin to fade. "What do you think Brayshaw'll do?"

Dan shrugged. "Man, I don't know if he can do anything."

"He's gone to bat for me before," Bucky reminded.

"Boy, I hope he can. I really got my heart set on playing ball."

Despite the situation, Bucky couldn't help but laugh. "Litton, you *always* got your heart set on playing something!"

At last Dan laughed. "Yeah, I know." He looked up at the darkening sky. "But, you know . . . last year you didn't play. It wasn't as much fun."

"Well, let's just see what Coach says tomorrow."

That evening he and Dad discussed the problem as they dug a trench line in the backyard for an additional sprinkler head. Daylight Savings Time was still two weeks away, but a huge floodlight bathed the grass in a twilight glow as they tugged at dirt clods and stray tree roots.

"I can't see your coach switching five games just for you two guys," Dad observed as he tossed another shovelful of dirt to the side. Flecks of wet soil stuck to his forearms as he paused for a breather.

"I know." Bucky grimaced. "He will if they let him, I think. But seems like every year it's more Friday night games than before."

Dad dropped to his knees and pulled at a twisted root. "Well, son, I admit that when you and your mom studied this whole church business I didn't really get excited about this Sabbath stuff." With a grunt he pulled the stubborn root free from the foot-deep trench. "But you've been faithful to your beliefs, and I know you're not going to switch now. The way it looks to me, being an Adventist . . ." For a moment he didn't seem to know what to say.

Bucky waited without speaking.

Mr. Stone looked at his son, affection written on his face. "Well, it hasn't done you any harm. That's all." He climbed to his feet. "You've done real good, Buck."

A lump came into the boy's throat. "Thanks."

The older man picked up the shovel. "Let's finish this later. Gettin' too dark out here."

The next day Bucky and Dan headed over to the athletic complex where Coach Brayshaw's office was. A bedraggled group of freshman boys were struggling through calisthenics in the gymnasium as the two juniors walked through. "Good old jumping jacks," Dan grinned as they went into the hallway leading to the coaching staff's office area.

"Come on in," Mr. Brayshaw beckoned as he saw them approaching. He had a worried look that Bucky spotted immediately.

"Not good news?"

The athletic director frowned. "Not good news." He ran his fingers through his hair. "I guess Dan showed you the schedule."

"Yeah." Bucky slipped into the chair next to the desk. "Lot of Friday nights."

"Can't the district switch them?" Dan tried to sound optimistic.

Coach Brayshaw sighed. "I've been on the phone with them three times," he muttered. "And the bottom line is—they might have been willing to switch one game. But five? No way."

"JV schedule only has four Friday nights," Dan pointed out.

"Yeah. But I wanted you fellows for varsity, of course." Coach looked from one to the other. "You two guys are the best I got."

A tiny glow filled Bucky at Brayshaw's comment. "What can we do?"

For a moment the man didn't answer. At last a little smile of irony came to his face. "Old Stevens asked me, 'Any chance your boys'll change their minds?' And I told him, 'Well, first of all, no way they're gonna change their minds, plus there's no way I even *want* them to change their minds.' " He paused to let the words sink in.

"Wow." Dan shook his head in disbelief. "That's . . ."

Coach Brayshaw pushed some papers to the side and leaned over his desk. "Look, you guys. I know how important your religion is to you. And you know how much the two of you mean to our chances of a varsity championship in baseball. But unless something big changes, I don't see any way out."

His intercom phone buzzed but he ignored it. "Mr. Stevens over at district—you remember him, Stone. He's the one who finally switched that basketball final a year ago. To Saturday night."

"Uh huh."

"I guess he took some real heat from State over that. Switching a final just for one player. Walker told me they had a review board meeting and everything later. So you can understand he got pulled pretty good from both sides."

Bucky winced. "I guess I never thought about that." He looked over at Dan.

"Anyway, that's where things are," Brayshaw said. "I should hear from Stevens by tomorrow, but I wouldn't bet a quarter on getting good news from him."

CHAPTER 2

TARGET PRACTICE

The soft orange glow of sunrise was just bathing the northern California hills behind Hampton Beach as Bucky finished his daily two-mile run. Slowing to a comfortable walk, he trudged up to the short brick wall outside his home and sank down for a brief rest. His pulse, although still racing slightly, began to slowly return to normal as he looked idly down the still-darkened residential avenue.

Despite the tranquil calm of early morning, the familiar baffled thoughts tugged at his mind. *Should I have gone to academy this year?* Except for the Dream Season basketball triumph, it had been a year of steady reminders that his Christian faith put him out of step with the rest of the world marching easily through life at Hampton High.

The baseball diamonds at the high school were empty as he pulled into the student parking lot. The closely cropped green grass and smooth dirt infields seemed to whisper their seductive invitation. Turning off the engine, he sat thinking.

"Come on, Stone! You're gonna be late."

He looked out of the Toyota's window to see Sam peering at him. "What are you daydreaming about in there?"

Bucky shrugged and motioned with his head toward the ballfield. "Baseball."

"Yeah, I heard." The Vietnamese boy nodded sympathetically. "Pretty much a Sabbath schedule, Dan was telling me."

"Yeah." Bucky shook his head. "I really wanted to play."

"Mr. Brayshaw can't just let you play in all the other games? And skip Friday nights?"

"Aaaah, that ain't fair to the team. You got to put the same nine guys out on the field every game if you're gonna win."

The senior nodded again. "What are you going to do?"

"What can I do? Just forget it, I guess." He looked up at Sam. "No band, no babes, no baseball. I mean, you know all about that."

Neither said anything for a moment. Both boys had been trumpet players in the band before becoming Adventists. Sam in particular had given up a coveted first-chair position rather than play for Friday night football games.

"Well," Sam said at last as he pulled his friend's door open, "it's only a game, man."

"Yeah."

During the lunch period Bucky and Dan went

over to the athletic department. Despite the gorgeous Bay Area weather, both boys had an ominous sense of what was ahead.

Sure enough. Coach Brayshaw motioned them into his office and gave them a dour look that told the whole story.

"Not too good, huh, Coach?"

The director snorted in frustration. "Well, I'll tell you what they said." His voice rose a little bit. " 'We ain't changing a single game from now on for any' "—he hesitated—" 'blank prayer meeting.' " The stark words hung in the air between them.

"Oh, come on," Dan protested. "It's not like that."

The coach looked over at him. "You're right, Litton," he admitted. "But like I was telling you, Stevens got flak from all sides last year for changing just one game. So this is just kind of a reaction to that."

Bucky sighed heavily, his mind working hard. "I don't know," he finally managed. "Seems to me like, you know, when we won the championship last week, and the reporters and all . . ." His voice trailed off. "You know, them writing about God and us winning and everything." He made a hopeful little gesture. "Didn't that help any?"

Mr. Brayshaw stared out the window, a little frown knitting his brow. Both boys waited.

At last he snapped back to look at them, leaning forward over his desk. "Look," he managed. "That kind of stuff turns some people *on* . . . and it turns some people *off*. You better just face that. And a guy like Stevens is just going to say, 'Listen, just play the game. We're here to run games, not some revival meeting.'" He scratched at his nose before continuing. "And from now on it's just gonna be 'play the game.' We got a schedule and there ain't no deviating from it for nothing."

"So where's that leave us?" Dan grumped.

The coach shrugged. "Well, leaves you cheerleadin' us from the sidelines, an' hoping that next year's schedule turns out better. Or . . ." He paused.

"What?"

Brayshaw hesitated. When he spoke it was with reluctance. "Playing on the frosh team."

Dan groaned. "The frosh team? Oh, for . . ." He looked over at Bucky.

"Sixteen-game schedule, all afternoons." The athletic director held out both hands hopefully. "And there ain't no guarantee that next year's varsity schedule's going to be any different. Friday night games are here to stay for the big boys."

"I know, but . . . " Dan's voice trailed off unhappily.

"We'll do it." Bucky spoke up abruptly, then glanced at his friend. "At least I will."

"Oh, come on, Buck. Frosh?"

"At least we're playin'. And look, we can really help the frosh team."

"Yeah, help them change their diapers." Dan struggled to his feet with a sour resentment written all over him. "I guess me too, Coach."

"I'm sorry," Brayshaw responded. "You know if there was anything I could do, I'd have done it by now." He looked at both of them. "I really wanted you fellows on the varsity team. But not if . . ." He reached into his desk drawer and pulled out two sheets of paper. "Here's the schedule for frosh."

"Thanks." Bucky took both schedules as the two boys walked out into the hallway. He glanced at one before offering it to Dan.

"Yeah, thanks a whole bunch." Dan wadded it up and stuffed it into his jeans pocket. "Man, Stone, this is just great, great, great!" He stalked toward the end of the hallway, then abruptly hit his fist against the concrete block wall before whirling around to face his teammate again. "Frosh team! Man, why don't we just go out for the stinking Chess Club? Or maybe the Tiddly-winks tournament? They don't have any games on Sabbath!"

Bucky took a step toward him. "Look, I don't like it any better than you do," he snapped. "But what else can we do?"

Dan looked at him, his eyes still smoldering. "This Sabbath stuff, Stone . . . is it going to mess us up like this our whole lives?" He took a deep breath. " 'Cause if it is . . ."

Bucky didn't answer. At the moment he wasn't sure what to say.

* * *

That night over a supper of cheese macaroni and salad he told Mom about the episode. "Is it really that much of a difference—I mean, varsity or this, what did you call it?"

"Frosh team?" Bucky set down his glass of cranberry juice. "Well, it's just like in basketball. The varsity team is the real thing. Frosh and even JV are just warmups. Every kid in school aims to get on varsity."

She nodded without speaking. Bucky toyed with the last bits of food on his plate. "I guess it kind of helps remind me that, you know, being a Christian is worth giving up something for."

After supper he went up to his room to work on a big batch of homework. Pulling several books out of his duffel bag, he suddenly groaned. "Where's the chemistry folder?"

Going out to the Toyota he searched through the front and back seats for the missing material. He even looked in the trunk although he knew it wouldn't be in there.

"Great!" he mumbled to Dad as he walked back into the house. "Stuff's due tomorrow, and I walked off and left everything at school like a fool."

"Going to go get it?"

Bucky shook his head. "Nah. I think I'll try to call Jonathan. He lives only about half a mile from here, I think."

The chunky chem partner answered on the first ring. "Yeh?"

"This is Bucky."

"Hey, how ya doin', Stone?"

"Not so good. I left all my stuff at school for chem."

"Bummer. It's all due tomorrow, boy."

"I know. Do you have your paperwork there?"

"Sure. I haven't done it yet."

Bucky took a breath. "OK if I come over and peek off yours?"

"Sure, I don't care. Come on over."

"I know sort of where you live, but you better give me the details." He quickly drew a rough sketch on the back of a piece of tattered napkin and took the stairs two at a time.

In the darkness it was hard to see where the little dirt road went off Route Two, but after missing it twice, Bucky finally pulled the Toyota into the cluttered front yard of Jonathan's house. The stocky junior turned on a porch light.

Bucky surveyed the crowded living room that had the appearance of an abandoned souvenir shop. "Man, what's all this stuff?"

"Oh, my folks collect everything in sight," the boy sighed, picking a path through the piles of lamps and jewelry. "My mom sort of does it as a paying hobby."

"You're kidding."

"Does pretty good at it too," the older boy grinned. "They're off bowling tonight. Every week."

He motioned Bucky into his surprisingly tidy bedroom. A large computer screen flickered with a random display of color cartoon characters. Pulling a folder out of the desk, he slapped it down on the bed. "Help yourself."

Bucky examined the data penned along the left-hand side of the lab report. "Man, you got this stuff down better than I did."

"Aaaah, I just copied it off old Smarty-pants herself." Jonathan sniffed. " 'Course we're all on the same team, so ain't no reason why we can't all use the same figures. Teacher said we could divide that up any way we wanted to."

Quickly Bucky recorded the data into his notebook and added the required conclusions, with Jonathan pointing out several suggestions as they worked together. In just over 20 minutes he had the assignment completed.

"Man, that's a relief," Bucky sighed, slapping his book shut. "Thanks a lot."

"No problem." Jonathan reached over and flipped a switch, watching as the computer's flickering images disappeared. He glanced up at a huge wall calendar. "Two more weeks till baseball season starts."

"A's fan, right?"

"Till the day I die. And, boy, I thought I *would* die the way those fools choked in the playoffs last year. Up three games to one and then, el-foldo. I'm still bleedin' over that one."

Bucky grinned. "How come you guys live out here in the dust and dirt instead of in town?"

"Oh, my folks like it out here. We moved here when I was about 5, and somehow the town's just never grown out this way. You live where? Over on . . ."

"Woodman Avenue."

"That's pretty nice houses over there."

"Yeah."

Jonathan bounded to his feet with a sudden burst of energy. "Come on, city boy. Let me show you something cool."

They went back into the clutter of the living room

and Jonathan went over to a wall cabinet. "Check this out."

He slid open a recessed drawer and pulled out a long black automatic pistol. Holding it up in the murky light of the room, he waved it in the air. "Not bad, huh?"

The younger student gaped. "Where'd you get that?"

Jonathan snorted. "My dad's got about five of 'em. I guess that's his hobby."

"What kind is it?"

With a smirk Jonathan rattled off a foreign-sounding name Bucky had never heard before. "We got a couple of twenty-twos and a huge old Magnum my dad keeps in the truck. But this baby's my favorite. Twelve shots a clip and it fires smooth, let me tell you."

Bucky gulped. "Would this kind of gun, you know, kill somebody if you . . ."

"Sure would. This ain't no Cracker Jacks prize, Stone, it's the real thing."

"You know how to use it?"

"Sure. Out here in the woods, who cares?" He slammed the drawer shut. "Come on."

Reluctantly Bucky followed the other boy outside. Rummaging around in the trash can next to the steps, Jonathan fished out a couple of tin cans and an empty bottle of pancake syrup. "We'll go for these."

Wordlessly Bucky watched as Jonathan set the three targets on the top rail of the fence circling the large front yard and driveway. With the tiniest swagger in his step, he paced back to the porch light where

Bucky waited. "OK, now, children," he intoned, "let's waste somebody."

Sighting along the barrel of the gun he squeezed the trigger. With a *pop* that seemed to echo right down the hill, the first can flew off the rail and landed a good eight feet away.

"Bingo." Lifting the pistol again he squinted and took aim at the syrup container. The second muffled report rang out in the darkness, but the target stayed perched on the rail.

"Missed it!" The chunky student muttered an oath and then turned toward Bucky. "Here you go."

"Oh, man, I don't know." Involuntarily he took a step backward.

"Come on."

"No, I really . . ." He shook his head. "I don't really want to."

Jonathan pursed his lips. "What's the big deal?"

Bucky glanced over at the fence railing where the second tin can and the syrup container were still visible in the moonlight. "I don't really like guns."

The other boy snorted. "You're just shooting at tin cans, man, not at helpless student nurses or something." He hefted the weapon and held it out again. "Don't worry, this won't turn you into the Terminator or Dirty Harry or anything."

With a sense of foreboding Bucky accepted the weapon. The metal felt cold and threatening in his sweating palm. "What do I do?"

Jonathan grinned. "You just look down the barrel of that baby and point and shoot. Safety's already off so you're ready to fire away."

Bucky stared at the automatic. "You're sure it's safe?"

The other boy began to laugh. "Yes, Bucky Boy, it's safe. As long as you point it at the can instead of at you or me."

"OK." A bit of resentment rising within him, Bucky stepped forward. Raising the pistol to eye level, he sighted at the tin can. The gun wavered in his grasp for a moment, but he waited until his nerves steadied enough to hold the target clearly in his sights.

Bam! The pistol kicked in his hand a little bit, but when he looked up the can was gone.

"Man, you nailed that sucker. Pretty good, Stone."

"Thanks." Bucky forced a nervous laugh. "Lucky beginner, I guess."

"We'll see." Jonathan motioned toward the syrup container. "Go for that one too."

This time Bucky didn't hesitate. Aiming carefully, he squeezed the trigger again. With a muted *thunk* the plastic bottle toppled over and spun in the dust.

Jonathan whistled. "Two for two. I guess I won't ever challenge you to a duel." He looked down at his ample stomach. "I'm too easy a target anyway."

Gingerly Bucky handed the weapon back to him. "Thanks." He could sense that his pulse was still racing.

"Anytime, man. You ever want to shoot target practice, just say the word. My folks are gone most of the time anyway."

"Yeah." Bucky glanced down at his watch. "I better get goin'."

As he drove down the little dirt road leading back to the highway, he looked in his rearview mirror at the country house still barely visible through the dust and moonlight. The excitement of shooting the pistol brought a guilty tingle to his skin.

CHAPTER 3

BASEBALL WEEKEND

It was a chilly afternoon as Dan and Bucky lined up with the freshmen and a few sophomore players for the first frosh drill. Scanning the rest of the would-be players, Bucky could see that several of the boys were well-built athletes.

"We may not even get on the starting lineup here," he muttered to Dan as they trotted laps after the first exercise routine.

"Aaaah, sure we will." Dan looked disdainfully at two freshmen passing him on the outer edge of the track. "Experience, man."

Bucky shook his head as they quickened their pace. "I haven't hardly done it since two years ago."

"Yeah, but we been hitting the batting cages all the last two weeks," the stockier athlete reminded.

A radio lying in the grass near the batting area crackled with the news that the A's were easily on their way to a fourth consecutive win to start the new season. "Hope we can do that good," Bucky grinned as he donned a batting helmet and took his place in the cage.

Despite the long time away from baseball, the hours of recent practice with the pitching machine paid off as he, batting both left- and right-handed, sent pitch after pitch rocketing into the outfield area. Several freshmen gathered around to watch the hitting display.

"Not bad, Stone," Dan whistled. "You may steal my Number Four spot in the lineup."

"No way. With your power?"

Waving the bat menacingly at the pitcher, Dan cocked his head. "Let 'er rip, Simpson."

"You got it." The first pitch whistled in right at thigh level. With a wicked *crack* of the bat Dan deposited the ball deep in left-center field. "Chew on that!" he hollered at the outfielders as they scrambled toward the fence.

"Looks like a triple from here," Coach Walker grinned. "Good poke, Litton."

"Thanks." Dan smiled in spite of himself. Baseball was still baseball!

After practice the two boys ambled casually back to the parking lot, not bothering to shower and change. In the distance Bucky could see Deirdre just climbing into her car. Both of them waved at her, but she gave just a casual nod of acknowledgment in response.

As Dan hummed a little tune that sounded like a funeral dirge, Bucky looked over at him without speaking.

"Can you give me a ride home?" Dan said all at once.

"What's the matter with your car?"

Dan kicked at a rock. "One of the cylinders isn't firing quite right, so I took it over to old Carlson this morning. Said he'd probably be done with it by tomorrow."

"Sure." Bucky fished in his duffel bag for the keys. "I guess I've owed you a few rides."

That night was a rare homework-free evening. After family worship Bucky plopped down with Rachel Marie to watch one of her favorite TV programs. He watched, bemused, as she chirped in delight about her favorite characters on the weekly show.

"I don't get it," he teased at one point. "What's so funny about that?"

She sighed impatiently. "You have to watch every week so you'll know what's going on. The bunny *always* does that."

"Bedtime." Mom poked her head into the living room. "Soon as that's done, kiddo."

The third-grader began to whine a protest but a pointed look from her mother quieted her.

Bucky gave his little sister a kiss and a quick squeeze as the final credits began to roll. "Good night, R.M."

"Who's that?"

"Short for Rachel Marie, dodo."

"Oh." She snickered. "Good night."

Dad lumbered into the living room and flopped down on the couch, propping both his feet up on the cushions. "Don't tell your mother."

Bucky picked up the TV remote control and flipped through the channels, setting it down again when an ESPN game came on. "Anything big down at work?"

His father shook his head. "Pretty quiet. With interest rates sneaking up again, the refinance craze is just about over."

A bases-loaded triple by one of the Colorado Rockies distracted his attention for just a moment. "Wow, they caught up just like that."

"Pretty good hit."

The next batter made the third out, and a Chevy commercial came on. Bucky turned to his dad, a question from the night before still nagging at him. "Dad, when you were over in Vietnam . . ."

His father raised an eyebrow. It was a topic that seldom came up in the Stone household.

"I mean, did you ever, you know, use a gun?"

His father swung his legs down and sat up straighter. "How come you want to know about that?"

"I just do." Bucky hit the mute button on the remote control and the huge color set fell silent. "Just because."

"Well, yeah, we all had guns," Dad told him. " 'Course, I was only in active combat for about four months. Right at the end."

"Were you in any, like, battles?"

"Just one." His dad's eyes seemed to cloud with the memory.

"What was it like?"

"Scary." Mr. Stone looked directly at his son. "It was real early in the morning, about five miles out from camp. A whole bunch of us ran into a nest of soldiers. Just kids, most of them. We shot at them, they shot back at us. We got about three of 'em, and the rest took cover. Then the helicopters came in and finished them off, and we got out of there."

"Did you . . ." Bucky wet his lips. "Did you kill any of them yourself?"

For a moment his father didn't answer. "I don't know," he said at last. "My buddy and I—there were two VC coming right at us. We both blasted away at them, and one of them went down. I don't know who hit him."

The stark words hung in the air. Bucky tried to imagine his father, just an 18-year-old teen barely older than himself, flat on his stomach in the steamy Vietnam jungles, firing a stream of bullets at enemy soldiers.

"Now come on," Dad prodded. "How come you want to know all about this?"

"Oh, I don't know." Without fanfare Bucky told his father about the target practice with Jonathan.

His father chewed on his lip. "Nothing wrong with guns, son, as long as they're used for the right thing."

"Like tin cans?"

Dad nodded. "Trouble is, a lot of people go crazy. They get themselves a shotgun just to, you know, 'defend themselves.' Or for target practice. But then they get into it." A pause. "Guns can be like that. And then one day . . ."

"What?"

Dad looked at him. "Well, then one day you read in the paper that some kid's been taken in for questioning. Shooting off his gun in the supermarket parking lot. Ten people dead. Stuff like that."

Bucky nodded, remembering the eerie sensation that followed the target practice and the little jolt of adrenalin that had come from just holding Jonathan's automatic in his hands for the first time. "Yeah, you're right," he admitted.

Reaching over, Mr. Stone punched his son lightly on the forearm. "You're a smart guy, Buck. Just don't let this Jonathan character talk you into anything dumb. Tin cans, that's it."

The following Tuesday afternoon Dan and Bucky powered the Panthers' frosh team to an easy 8-1 victory over the Spartans. The home team's pitcher was a tough little competitor, stingy with hits and walks, and the two juniors had three hits apiece.

"Well, so we're big shots on the baby team," Dan shrugged with a grin. The left fielder had made two dazzling catches in the field and was glowing in spite of himself.

"Yeah, you had yourself a game," Bucky admitted, reaching in his pocket for the keys to his car. "You keep playing like that . . ." His voice trailed off.

"Yeah, there ain't nowhere for us to go." A tiny frown returned. "You and me could bat a thousand each, and still it wouldn't get us anywhere."

Bucky gave a little hop to miss a huge pothole in the faded pavement. "Hey, so we witness here on frosh. Just like always. We play our best for God and give Him the glory."

"Yeah, I know." Dan nodded his reluctant agreement. "You and me, Stone."

"Really." Bucky waved goodbye to his friend and eased himself into the bucket seat of the little white Toyota.

Just as he turned the ignition key, a large form blocked his view. "Hey, Stone, where are you running off to?"

"How's it going, Jonathan?" Bucky grinned at the sight of his chemistry partner.

"Not bad. You guys win today?"

"Yup. Eight-zip. Oh, I guess they got one run in that last inning. But we creamed 'em pretty good."

"You been keepin' an eye on our Oakland A's?"

"What, six in a row now?"

"That's right." Jonathan pumped both fists in the air. "They keep goin' like this, we're going to go 162 and oh this season."

"Oh, right." Bucky laughed as he turned off his engine.

"Listen, Stone, I got an idea."

"If it involves beating Tracy in the next chem test, count me in," Bucky grinned.

"Are you kidding? How are you going to do better than a hundred?"

"Yeah, I guess we're never going to catch her."

"Anyway, this is better." The stocky student paused for effect. "A's and Seattle. Three straight games."

"When?"

"This weekend, man. Friday, Saturday, Sunday."

"Man, that's a lot of running down to Oakland."

A big grin spread across the other boy's face. "Who said anything about Oakland? I'm talking about Washington State and the Kingdome, my friend. You and me in Seattle, smack dab in the middle of enemy territory, cheering for the A's in front of those poor Mariner fans as we stuff 'em three in a row."

The news took Bucky by surprise. "Huh?"

Jonathan pulled out an already worn baseball schedule. "We leave after school on Thursday, get about two-thirds of the way. Friday there ain't no school here anyway because of state inspection. We roll into town by noon for a nothing-but-baseball weekend."

"Can we get tickets?"

Jonathan emitted his usual hoarse chuckle. "In the Kingdome? Are you kidding? That place holds about two million fans at a time, and the M's can't hardly draw enough of a crowd to do a decent wave."

Bucky laughed. "I guess I'd have to check with my folks, but it sounds pretty good to me." A sudden thought struck him. "Hey, wait a minute. Friday and Saturday? What time are the games?"

Jonathan gave a knowing nod. "Yeah, yeah, Mr. Holy." The tone in his voice was light. "I figured you'd be askin' me that before too much time. Friday's a day game, Saturday night at 7:00 p.m., Sunday at 1:00." He grinned. "See, Stone, I even got the church's blessing for you."

The taller boy nodded. "Wow. I guess you did." He thought for a moment. "I can't go Saturday night until after sundown. Which might be about 7:15."

"That's cool." Jonathan wasn't about to be deterred. "So what about it, boy? Baseball marathon weekend and a ten-game streak of W's?"

"Where are we going to stay?"

Jonathan folded up his A's schedule and reverently put it in his wallet. "My uncle lives just north of Seattle. 'Bout eight miles from the Kingdome. We can stay with him."

Bucky started up the engine again. "OK. I'll let you know for sure tomorrow, but go ahead and put me down. I got to change my shift at the bank, but that should be easy."

"All right, Stone!" Jonathan reached through the open window and gave his chemistry partner a high five. "A's rule. And Panthers, too," he added.

"Right."

Jonathan began to walk away, then suddenly turned back. "I may get a couple of other kids to go too," he added. "So we can split gas up four ways and stuff. We'll go in my van."

"OK." Bucky watched, bemused, as Jonathan lifted his considerable bulk into a faded maroon van with a huge green A's logo pasted on the side. Although Bucky was more of a Giants fan, the idea of a blockbuster weekend of baseball sounded fun. And rooting for the A's in Seattle territory would be a hoot.

Suddenly a light bulb went on in his brain. *Lisa's in Seattle!*

CHAPTER 4

OFF TO A HOT START

Tingling with renewed excitement, Bucky decided to stop by Sam's house on the way home to share the news. He pulled to a stop in front of the condominium complex where the Minh family lived. Ringing the doorbell, he listened for the soft padding of footsteps inside.

Sam's mother, a short woman, recognized Bucky from earlier visits. "Yes, Sam, he is here," she intoned in her careful English. "Wait, please." She turned and went to the stairway and called out in Vietnamese.

A moment later Sam appeared. "Hey, Stone, how's it goin'?" He came over to the front door and slipped on a pair of sneakers. On each of Bucky's earlier visits he had detected just a hint of tension that indicated Sam's parents were still uncomfortable with visitors.

The two boys walked out to the street where Bucky had parked the Toyota. With a grin he told Sam about the proposed trip to Seattle.

"So you're going to get together with Lisa again?" Sam got the point immediately.

Bucky reddened. "Yeah, I figured I'd try."

Sam laughed. "Man, with the luck you've been having, she'll probably be off at some flower show for the whole weekend."

"I know," Bucky confessed. "I haven't had a chance to even call her yet."

"Well, I hope you guys get together." Sam reached into his pocket and pulled out a pack of gum. "You want some?"

Bucky shook his head. "How're your folks doing?" he asked.

The older boy shrugged. "Good, I guess. I mean, they still pretty much like to keep to themselves. Guess you can tell."

"Hey, that's OK." For a moment a picture of Vasana and her Oriental reserve popped into his mind.

"You and that what's-his-name doing OK in chemistry?"

Bucky laughed. "Jonathan? That guy's too much. Yeah, we're getting by. 'Course, we'll never catch up to Tracy."

"Tracy . . . Tracy . . ." Sam's forehead knit in thought. "Hey, wait a minute! I know who that is. Real short girl, red hair, right?"

"Yup."

Sam shook his head. "Man, that chick's got brain power like you wouldn't believe."

"Tell me about it." Bucky rubbed his baseball

pants against a mud spot on the car's fender. "Half the time she tells the teacher how to do the homework."

"Yeah, I had her last semester in Science Fair competition," the older boy observed. "She put together some crazy thing on computer language translations, had it all tracked out on a laser printer and everything. Seems like somebody told me she even got it printed up in a magazine or something." He laughed. "That lady's dangerous, Stone."

Bucky grinned. "Yeah, I'm never going to come in any better than second as long as she's at Hampton High."

Suddenly Sam's face lit up. "Hey, guess what I heard yesterday." He pointed a finger at his friend. "I saw Pastor Jensen at Albertson's, and he told me that Miss Cochran is taking Bible studies with him."

The news left the younger student stunned. "Are you kidding? Really?"

"I guess they just got started."

"Wow." Bucky felt his pulse jump a beat. "I mean, she came to church a few times, but then for about a month I didn't see her there. I didn't really want to, you know, bug her or anything. Her being a teacher and everything."

"Well, she and Jensen are going to go right through it. Once a week, he told me. I guess that funeral business really got to her."

"That's terrific. Here I've been praying for her, and now . . ."

That evening at supper he told his parents about it. "Oh, honey, that's really good news." Mom came around the table and gave Bucky a hug. Even Dad gave his son a little nod of approval.

But the Seattle trip met with considerably less enthusiasm. "How long a drive is it up there?" Mom wanted to know.

Bucky tried to remember. "I guess maybe 10 or 11 hours."

"And this Jonathan guy is the one you were telling me about the other night?" Dad asked.

"Yeah." Bucky gulped, remembering that his mother hadn't heard about the target shooting. Quickly he gave her the bare details.

She frowned. "Oh, Bucky, I don't know about this, then. You know what I think about guns."

As an awkward silence set in, Rachel Marie glanced from her parents to her brother with a third-grader's curiosity. "Where are you going anyway, Bucky?"

"To Seattle," he responded, a little edge creeping into his voice. "Look, it'll be fine. We'll be with his uncle the whole time. There'll be two other guys along and everything. I mean, he's basically a nice kid. He and his folks just have different, you know, hobbies and stuff."

His father took a sip of coffee before answering. "Well, you know what I told you before. People want to keep a gun in their home, there's nothing wrong with that. Just as long as it's only used for what it's supposed to be used for. I just get real tired of seeing on CNN News about some dummy who lost his head with some gun his daddy had up in the attic." He set down his coffee cup and gave Bucky a meaningful glance, then added, "What's this going to cost?"

His son shrugged. "I dunno. Three tickets, plus I've got to help with gas and stuff like that. Maybe one motel split four ways." He looked at Dad. "$75, maybe."

"Well, you're on your own, sport," Mr. Stone said with a small grin. "I guess I don't care if you go, but you've got that big-time job down at the bank. You can pay for your own spring break trips."

The last remark about spring break didn't make Mom any happier, Bucky could tell. But finally, after several more questions were discussed and answered, she gave a reluctant nod. "I know we can trust you, honey. That's the main thing."

After supper he went into the living room and picked up the phone. The familiar female voice came on the line after just the first ring.

"This is your friend Mr. Stone from California," he announced.

Lisa laughed. "Well, Mr. Stone, what a happy moment this is. How are you?"

"OK." He gulped. "I've decided I need to come and see how *you* are."

A long pause. "I hope this time you really mean it."

"Hey," he retorted. "It was you who flew off to Florida last time, leaving me with tearstains on my pillow."

"Oh, yeah." She laughed. "Well, when are you coming?"

"How about this weekend?" He held his breath, waiting for her response.

"Oh, no," she muttered. "I don't think . . ."

His heart sank. "What?"

"I don't think I have anything at all planned this weekend," she laughed. "So how am I going to get rid of you?"

In the growing April twilight he silently pumped his fist in the air. *All right!*

"What time do you think you'll get up here?" she wanted to know, her voice revealing her own excitement.

"It's all kind of sudden," he admitted. "I'm riding up with a friend of mine from chemistry class and a couple of other guys. And we'll be getting there just in time for the Friday afternoon game. So you better just let me call you when I can get free. For sure we'll go to church together Sabbath and stuff. I don't know about maybe the Saturday night and Sunday games. If Jonathan has tickets already or what. Maybe you can come to those with me." He laughed. "Give me a chance to show you off in front of the guys."

"OK." She gave her characteristic little laugh. "I'll just sit here with my hand poised over the receiver. So don't break my heart again."

"I promise." They visited for a few more minutes before he hung up.

The next day in chemistry lab the little redhead was absent. "Where's Miss High IQ?" Bucky wondered.

"Sick, I guess," Jonathan shrugged. "You and me got to do all the work ourselves for a change." Scowling, he peered into the chemistry manual. "Just hope we don't stink up the place with the wrong formula or something." He tied his white apron strings, muttering as one of them knotted up on him. "I'll pour in all the goop, you write down the numbers." As he turned on a burner he hissed softly to himself. "Or just make something up. We'd probably come out better that way."

Bucky pulled out his pen and wrote the date on the top of the sheet. "You ready for all that baseball?"

"Sure am." Jonathan squinted as he measured out the grainy black powder. "Got the tickets all ordered at 'Will Call' and everything."

Bucky was going to ask about an extra ticket for Lisa when a sudden *pouff!* of unexpected smoke startled both boys. "What was that?" he exclaimed.

Jonathan began to wave a towel in the air. "Rats! Too much sodium nitrate." He glared at several other students who held their noses in mock protest at the rancid smell coming from the two boys' table.

"Great! I always wanted to be popular," Bucky grunted, ignoring the glares of the others.

"Well, quick, write down something. 'Doubling recipe leads to immediate barnyard atmosphere.'" Jonathan laughed.

"What time do we head out tomorrow?" Bucky tried to change the subject.

The stocky boy shrugged. "I figure the sooner we can leave after lunch the better. I only got one English class, and I don't mind skipping it."

Bucky nodded. "Yeah, I think I can make that."

"Bring some bucks for gas and stuff," Jonathan advised. "And motel. Tickets were $9.00 each."

"We need motel money both ways?"

The other boy shook his head as he measured out

three cc's of the catalyst compound. "I figure after Sunday's game we'll just bomb right home. Get here 2:00 in the morning or so, but that way we won't miss Monday's classes."

That afternoon after school Bucky and Dan drove together to Kennedy High School for their second frosh contest. They couldn't help but smile to themselves as they saw some of the freshman antics in the outfield. Kennedy, in particular, had a disorganized crew, including a shortstop who appeared to be all of 13 years old.

Still, it was a tightly played contest, with the Kennedy hurler fooling even Dan on close pitches. Twice in a row Hampton High's leading slugger went down on strikes.

"Little weasel," he muttered to Bucky as the two trotted out to the field for the bottom of the sixth, holding onto a slim one-run lead.

"Hang in there," Bucky laughed. "You got one more chance for revenge."

In the top of the seventh and final frame the first two Panthers reached base before Bucky came to bat. Watching the ball carefully, he let a close 3-2 pitch go by for ball four. Bases loaded!

"Come on, Stone, hit those close ones," Coach Walker chided as the junior trotted down to first base. "We aren't paying you and Litton to walk." Bucky noted a tone of teasing in his voice.

"I just wanted to let Dan have his chance," Bucky answered. Moments later he leaped in the air as the tiny white sphere whistled in a mammoth arc toward center field. "Grand slam!" he hollered in triumph as the four hitters circled the bases. He stood at home plate to welcome the grinning Litton. "Not a bad swat, boy!"

"Thanks!" Dan looked up at the sky as if to acknowledge that all accounts were squared. "I guess I feel better now."

"Funny how that works," his teammate grinned, giving Dan a vintage Oakland forearm bash. Bucky drove home after the contest savoring a warm mixture of triumph and anticipation over the upcoming trip to Seattle and one Washington State junior named Lisa Nichols.

CHAPTER 5

SURPRISE COMPANIONS

Thursday morning Bucky headed for school with a duffel bag filled with clothes and $100 in his wallet. Despite her earlier reservations, Mom managed to give him a cheerful send-off for the Seattle trip.

"You behave yourself, young man," she teased as she tucked a stash of goodies into his already over-stuffed bag.

"I will," he managed with a mouthful of syrupy waffles.

It was a fantastic mid-April morning, promising a quick and easy trip north. During a classroom break Dan gave him a Panthers-two-and-oh high five in the hallway. "Pretty good shot yesterday," Bucky told him again. "Grand slammeroo!"

"Yeah." Dan brightened. "Thanks!" He gave his friend a comradely pop on the shoulder. "You guys heading out right after lunch?"

"Actually, right before, I think." Bucky slammed his locker door shut with a clang. "Gives us an extra hour on the road."

"Hey, listen, have a good time."

"Man, you should have come along."

"Naaah." Dan shook his head. "I'm behind in about three subjects. Plus I got work all day tomorrow with there bein' no school."

"Bummer."

"I'll watch for you on TV though," Dan interjected. "Three straight wins, promise?"

"Yeah."

"OK, then. Tell Lisa hi for me."

"Sure. And you be sure to look for Miss Cochran at church Sabbath."

The stocky ballplayer nodded. "Oh, that's right. I'll keep an eye out for her."

Right at noon Bucky headed out to the parking lot. Digging his bag out of the Toyota's little trunk, he carefully locked all the doors and looked around for the big maroon van.

"Hey! Stone! Over here." With a harsh blast of his horn, Jonathan rolled to a stop next to the tall junior. "Hop in." He reached over awkwardly to release the sliding passenger door.

Bucky tossed his bag onto the already crowded van floor and climbed in, looking up to see who the other passengers were. *What in the . . .*

"Do you know Jill?" Jonathan spoke in a half-shout over the din of the van's huge stereo system. He nodded toward a strange girl with medium-length black hair. "I believe you already know Miss Tracy Givenchy."

Bucky was at a loss for words. The redhead snickered at the expression on his face. "Come on in, Mr. Stone. We won't bite."

The tall boy gulped. "I . . . I guess I didn't know who you were bringing along," he managed, looking up to the front seat where Jonathan was already maneuvering out of the high school parking lot.

"Any objections?" Tracy scooted over in the passenger bench seat to make room for him.

"Well, I guess not." His mind raced, trying to think of something clever to say. "You're prettier than who I imagined Jonathan might come up with."

Her face lit up. "Why, Mr. Stone. So gallant!" She fluttered her eyelashes at him. "You really think I'm cuter than that guy Litton you hang around with?"

Bucky gulped. "Well, I've always been partial to . . ."

A grumpy oath from the front seat interrupted the conversation. "Missed it!" The van lurched to a stop at a yellow light that had just turned red. "I hate when I decide to zoom through, and the guy in front of me makes up his mind to stop instead." Rolling down his window, he stuck his head out. "Fathead!"

Jill, in the front seat next to Jonathan, reached out and turned down the van's cassette stereo. "Ease up," she complained. "We got all day."

Bucky felt his heartbeat racing. The discovery of two girls in the van put a whole new face on the Seattle expedition. Two guys and two girls—and a four-day road trip. What would Mom and Dad have said if they'd known? A glance at Jonathan's owlish face in the mirror gave him a clue that his friend had held back on purpose.

He turned to Tracy. "When . . . when did you decide to come along?"

She shrugged. "Jonathan invited me the other day, so I said sure."

"Do you like baseball?"

"I guess." She popped a bubble with her gum. "I did a report in eighth grade about baseball statistics and stuff like that. So, yeah, I watch once in a while when I've got time."

The on-ramp to I-5 came up on the right and Jonathan revved the big V-8 engine to squeal past a black 300-ZX onto the freeway. Despite his still startled mental state, Bucky laughed. "There ain't no rush," he said, raising his voice so the driver could hear him.

"Did you have your lunch yet?" Tracy asked.

"Huh uh. How about you?"

"Nope. Me neither. Jonathan dragged me out of history right at noon. What have you got?"

"Oh, my mom packed me some stuff." He pulled out his duffel bag and began to inspect its contents. "I guess I'll get by."

Tracy reached into her purse and pulled out a baggie with a small sandwich in it. "Sick! Salami again." She took a bite of it and made a face. "That's all we had in the fridge this morning."

Bucky fished through his own bag and pulled a sandwich free. For a moment he hesitated. In the front seat Jonathan and Jill were munching out of a big bag of green onion and sour cream-flavored potato chips.

" 'Scuse me," he murmured to Tracy. Bowing his head, he said a short silent prayer before taking a bite.

The redhead gave him a quizzical look. "What, you pray before lunch every day?"

He couldn't tell if her voice had any trace of derision in it or not. "Yeah," he nodded, trying to sound casual.

"Hmmmm." She shrugged and took another bite. "That's good, I guess." She looked down at her own sandwich. "How's that go? 'God is great, God is good, uh . . . let us eat up all the food.' Is that right?"

Swallowing, he managed to clear his throat. "How about you? I mean, church and stuff like that?"

Tracy shook her head, her short red curls jiggling. "My mom likes to get us to go at Easter and stuff like that. I guess she goes to mass maybe once a month."

"She's Catholic?"

A shrug. "Well, yeah, I guess I am too. Kind of." She popped the lid of a Pepsi can and took a long swallow, then held out the container. "Want some?"

"No thanks."

They chatted as the miles of northern California freeway rolled past. Bucky finished off his lunch and even managed to share a piece of carrot cake with her. "Not bad," she grinned, wiping away a stray crumb.

He took advantage of a break in the music din as Jonathan fished in the glove compartment for yet another hard-rock cassette. "So how come you're so smart?" he asked in a mock-complaining voice. "Makes it tough for Jonathan and me to keep up."

Her lips formed a tiny pout. "Poor boys. I don't want to hurt your feelings."

"Come on," he remonstrated. "You're getting all those A's on purpose."

She nodded. "It's just always been so easy," she admitted. "I mean, I got a B once in sixth grade. That was it."

Bucky whistled. "One B? In your life?"

"Yeah."

He had to laugh. "I never heard of anybody getting only one B their whole life. Wow!"

She reached out and daintily kicked at his shin. "Well, you're doing OK. Decent grades, basketball hero. Could be a baseball hero too, from what everybody says, except for some church thing where you can't play—what, Saturdays?"

"Uh huh."

"Plus you aren't the most ugly guy in school," she added, her voice a little bit softer. Suddenly she seemed less cocksure.

"Now I'm blushing," he grinned.

"Well, let's see," Tracy mused. "You're six foot four, and I'm four eleven on a real good day. Yep, I see real possibilities there, Mr. Stone." Again she batted her eyelids at him.

Bucky felt a shiver go up his spine. In the front seat Jonathan and Jill were engrossed in a meaningless argument about the age of some rock group's lead singer. A slow, bluesy love song began to play as he turned his attention back to Tracy, who was eyeing him, curiosity written all over her face.

Suddenly a kind of panic gripped his heart. *Lisa!*

The presence of the little redhead had temporarily caused him to forget that another young woman was eagerly waiting for him at the other end of his excursion.

Tracy cocked her head to one side. "What's the matter? All of a sudden you looked like you choked on a Twinkie."

"No . . . nothing," he stammered. "I just was thinking of something I forgot."

She reached out and nudged him again. "Well, don't worry, sweetie. If you forgot any of your home-work, I'll personally help you with it when we get back home. Deal?"

Again Bucky felt his face flush. How could he keep a lid on things during the long ride to Seattle? And how could he get away now to be with Lisa? Was Tracy really interested in him . . . or was he imagining it?

The van tires squealed as Jonathan swerved to cut between two cars. The maroon vehicle was easily outdistancing every other car on the road. Bucky strained to peer at the speedometer that looked like it was registering nearly 80 miles an hour.

"Goin' too fast for you?" Tracy, sitting closer now, murmured. She covered her mouth as a yawn threat-ened to escape. "Boy, this warm weather is making me sleepy. You don't mind if I take a nap?"

"No." Bucky still didn't trust his voice.

"Turn down the music, Jonathan!" Tracy pulled her legs up onto the seat and leaned over until her head was resting lightly on Bucky's shoulder. "Wake me up when it's suppertime, sweetie."

"I, uh, sure." Bucky's heart sank. *This was trouble!*

CHAPTER 6

PIT STOP

The mid-afternoon glare through the left windows hit Bucky in the face as the maroon van hurtled at high speed up I-5. Tracy, dozing lightly, shifted around in the passenger seat to shield her eyes. A stray lock of her short red hair threatened to tickle his nose, and she murmured a sleepy apology as she brushed it away.

Casting a glance at the couple's reflection in the driver's rearview mirror, Jonathan's dancing eyes seemed to betray his amusement. He raised an eyebrow at Bucky's helpless expression and flashed a big grin as he reached over and hit a different button on the stereo. A slow romantic hit began to quietly throb through the rear speakers.

"Mmmmmm. My favorite." Tracy stirred for a moment and slid a bit closer to Bucky. Without seeming to mean to, her left hand edged over until it rested next to his arm.

Bucky gazed resolutely out of the right-hand windows, trying to avoid the harsh rays of the sun. They were well north of the Sacramento area now and the smooth bands of freeway stretched ahead of them with just a few other cars dotting the expanse of road. Jonathan, seemingly intent on setting a Hampton High speed record to Seattle, was passing everybody in sight.

"If you get a ticket you're on your own," Bucky said quietly, hoping not to wake Tracy.

"Aaaah, no way. They don't patrol around here much," the stocky driver retorted. "Anyway, I got Jill doin' lookout for me."

The other girl popped open a can of soda and took a tiny sip. "Don't count on it," she laughed. "With you doing 85, by the time I can spot a car we're already by 'em." She nudged Jonathan lightly. "Maybe you ought to slow down a little bit at least. This thing probably doesn't get that great gas mileage even rolling downhill with the engine off."

Despite the redhead's tiny size, Bucky could feel his left arm beginning to go numb. Squirming gingerly, he tried to shift positions without awakening her.

In the front passenger seat Jill swiveled around to face them. "I heard you and Litton are just playing on the frosh team this year."

"Yeah." He nodded. "We couldn't, uh . . ." He tried to think. "Well, I guess it was just scheduling problems. Otherwise, we'd probably be on the varsity team."

Suddenly he realized how his last remark must have sounded. "I mean, that's what Brayshaw had said he wanted us for."

"What is it anyway? You can't play Saturdays or something?"

Again Bucky nodded. "Yeah. Because of church." He peeked down at the top of her head, but the redhead wasn't stirring. "A while ago Dan and I both became Adventists, and they keep Sabbath—you know, like Sunday—from Friday evening until Saturday evening."

The dark-haired girl gave a thoughtful little nod. "It's really that big a deal?"

He chewed on his lip. "Well, I guess to us it is. I know everybody doesn't see it that way. I mean, obviously not. But when I got into it I just—I don't know—decided 'that's what God asks me to do, so I'll do it.'"

Jill looked over at Jonathan, but he was intent on passing two huge semis blocking the left lanes. Taking another swallow of her drink, she wiped her lips. "I guess most of the kids at school just never get into stuff like that," she observed. "I don't know why."

"How about you?"

A little shrug. "Me neither, I guess. I mean, with school and volleyball and, you know, things like this, I never . . ."

"Do your folks ever, like, go to church?"

She shook her head. "I live with my grandmother. My folks split up with I was in third grade. Then my mom ended up on probation for tax fraud a long time ago, so that's where I wound up." She gave another of her little shrugs.

"Man, that's too bad." Bucky thought of the stability of his own comfortable home life. Even living with parents with different spiritual perspectives, he still enjoyed the privileges of a complete family.

A sudden blast of rock music seemed to knock the whole van into the next lane. Tracy jerked awake with a stunned little yelp.

"What's the big idea?" Despite the jarring interruption Bucky began to laugh. "What's wrong with you, Shultz?"

"Hey, I like this song." Beating on the steering wheel in time to the heavy beat, he began to sing along in a horrible baritone.

"Help!" Tracy held her hands over her ears. "Now I hope the cops *do* pull us over. Anybody sings like that oughta be arrested."

The song came to the chorus, and Jonathan cranked up his own singing a notch, bouncing his ample frame back and forth in the protesting bucket seat. Jill, laughing so hard she had tears in her eyes, reached down for an empty potato chip bag that she wadded up and threw at the driver. He swerved slightly, then fumbled for the bag and tossed it back.

Mercifully, the song finally ended and an insistent advertisement for a waterbed warehouse came on. Sighing heavily, Jonathan reached out and switched the stereo off. "OK, I'll give you critical people a break."

"We're not critical, just discriminating," Tracy

observed. She looked over at Bucky. "Thanks for being my pillow."

He forced a grin. "That's OK."

In the front seat Jill pointed down the freeway. "There's a rest stop coming up. How about giving us feminine people a five-minute break to freshen ourselves up?"

"I vote yes," Tracy put in.

Obediently Jonathan pulled into the slow lane and edged off the freeway into the small wooded park. After a short break the two girls emerged from the restroom, both laughing about something. Jonathan gave his partner an amused look and shrugged.

"Hey, you picked 'em," Bucky laughed.

"I don't see you complaining."

As the van rumbled back onto the freeway, Bucky cocked an ear. With the music off, he suddenly detected a strange sound.

"What's that clicking noise?"

Jonathan motioned the two girls to be quiet and strained to listen as the van resumed its usual speed. "What? I don't hear nothin'."

"That kind of . . . can't you hear it? There! Tick tick tick."

"Yeah, I hear it too," Jill piped up. "Something's the matter, Jonathan."

"There's a couple of gas stations at the next exit," Bucky announced as a roadside sign flashed by. "Maybe we better at least fill up. Then you could have somebody listen."

"I still don't hear anything," Jonathan retorted, but

he began to slow down again with a grumble to himself.

Suddenly the sound became more pronounced. "Ooooh. What *is* that?" Tracy looked behind her at the freeway behind the car.

"What are you looking for?" Bucky asked.

"See if there's smoke or something."

The maroon van pulled to a labored stop at the self-serve pump. Sighing to himself, Jonathan hoisted the short hood and went in search of an attendant. Climbing out of the passenger door, Bucky headed to the front of the van and peered into the confusing tangle of parts and wires. A moment later Tracy stood next to him. "Have you fixed it yet?"

He gave a short laugh. "Honey, you are looking at the greatest single glaring weakness in my résumé. Car engines." He pointed down at a grease-smeared handle. "I think you check the oil with that thing there, but that's about it for me."

A short Black man in a Shell service outfit walked up with Jonathan. "What have we got here, folks?" Bucky stepped aside to let him look. The man took a quick scan of the engine and nodded with a muttered grunt to himself.

"What's wrong? You see anything?" The usually cheerful Jonathan's face was suddenly sober.

"Yeah, there it is." The man pointed. "Belt right there just shredded itself." He reached down and fingered it. "Yep, it's shot." He turned to Jonathan. "That—and this one here really should be changed too. You fix one without the other, you're just throwin' your money out the window."

Shaking his head, Jonathan snapped off an angry epithet. "How much is it?"

The man wiped his hands on his already stained trousers and scratched at his chin. "I'll have to check the chart inside, but I think the two of 'em will run you right at about $40. Might be a bit less or a bit more, but that's close. 'Course, I'll have to see if we even have them in here."

"You can't just do the one?"

The attendant shrugged. "Well, sure, I could. But unless you're going right home, you really need to do them both right now."

Jonathan sagged. "We're goin' clear up to Seattle and then back to the Bay Area."

"Well, that's it then."

The stocky boy pounded a fist against the side of the van. "Man, that really cuts into the cash."

"Look," Bucky offered. "I'll help you with it."

"You got some extra?"

The taller student shook his head. "Not a lot," he confessed. "But what else are we gonna do?"

Finally Jonathan gave an exasperated little nod. "Man, thanks. When we get up to Seattle I can get some extra bucks there."

The attendant emerged from the station, shaking his head. "We haven't got these belts in stock, but I just called over to the auto supply store, and they've got some. But it'll be about an hour."

Jonathan's scowl grew deeper. "All I can say is, those A's better win all three games." He nodded to the attendant. "Yeah, I guess, go for it. I ain't got no choice."

The long minutes ticked by slowly in the late April afternoon. Tracy, balancing her petite self on a raised section of concrete edging next to the Shell station, managed to walk from one end to the other without slipping off. "Pretty cool, huh?" she bragged to Bucky.

"Not bad."

At last she tipped off to the right. Cocking her head to one side, she shielded her eyes. "Hey, I think there's an ice-cream store down there."

"Where?"

"See?" She gave a bubbly little laugh. "Come on!"

Tagging after her, he wondered if it would be difficult to get away to see Lisa in Seattle. And what was he supposed to do with this maddeningly brilliant redhead?

"Well, it's not 31 flavors," Tracy said as they arrived, "but at least they got a few."

"Are you going to have some?"

"For sure." She began to fish in the pocket of her shorts. "How about you?"

He shook his head, remembering the yet unpaid repair bill. "I better not."

"Oh, come on. I'm buying."

He laughed. "Well, in that case, I'll have a triple banana split with twenty toppings on it."

"Ha ha." Ordering for both of them, she handed him an oversized cone. "Since you guys are buying belts with your fun money, I guess I can pay for this."

"Thanks." He took a healthy bite. "What's that kind you got?"

"Fudge peanut butter." She held out her cone. "Here."

"No, that's OK."

"Come on." Pulling on his arm, she finally got the cone up to tasting level. "You'll like it."

They traded tastes all the way back to the service station, where Jonathan leaned against the van with a sour expression. "I hope you brought enough for everybody," he said when he saw the nearly consumed cones.

"Sorry." Tracy slipped her hand into the crook of Bucky's arm. "Just me and my baseball hero."

A good hour and a half had elapsed before the new belts finally arrived, and it was growing dark by the time the attendant finally signaled for Jonathan to start up the engine. After a momentary sputter, the engine roared to life.

"That's more like it," the attendant nodded. "That should get you folks up to your ball game."

Fishing in his wallet for the cash, Jonathan accepted $20 from Bucky and handed the bills over with a small sigh. "Come on, let's roll," he muttered, pulling himself back into the driver's seat.

"You still going to try to make it to Portland tonight?" Seated for the moment in the front passenger seat, Bucky looked for a mileage marker.

Jonathan shook his head with a frustrated glance at the digital clock on the dashboard. "Man, no way. It'd be after midnight before we got up there." He shrugged. "Maybe Medford."

"What about supper?"

"Yeah, I know. You guys hungry yet?" He adjusted his seatbelt. "We really need to make up some time before we stop again."

"Sure." The ice cream had put off hunger pains for the moment. "But keep your eyes open." Bucky forced a laugh. "For something cheap."

Jonathan seemed about to say something, then abruptly stopped. A moment later he gave a distinct little laugh. "Well, if we run out of cash, I guess I can always think of a way to get more." His voice was suddenly quiet.

The odd remark mystified Bucky. "What are you talking about, Shultz?"

A slow grin spread across the other boy's face. Reaching over, he released the glove compartment door. There, lying underneath a pile of old road maps, lay the gleaming black automatic.

CHAPTER 7

A GUN IN THE GLOVE BOX

Involuntarily Bucky sucked in his breath. "What is that thing doing here?" Instinctively he reached out and flipped up the little door, almost clipping his friend's fingers.

"Watch it!"

Bucky turned around to see if the girls had noticed, but they were involved in an animated backseat conversation. He turned back to Jonathan. "Are you crazy, man? Bringing that along?" He kept his voice low, trying to mask his disgust.

"Hey, it's no biggie. Lighten up." Jonathan flipped the radio on again and began hunting for a clearer FM signal. "I just like to have it around. Make's me feel good."

"What for?" The whispered words had a harshness to them as Bucky shook his head impatiently.

"What are you going to shoot at?" He gestured toward the front windshield at the twilight scenery. "Cows?"

The stocky driver shot Bucky an impatient look. "Don't be stupid. I'm not going to blast away at nothing. As I said, I just . . . like having it around. Just in case."

His cheeks flushing, Bucky glanced over his shoulder, but the girls were still oblivious to the tense confrontation in the front seat. Leaning closer to the other boy, he muttered in a low tone, "Well, just keep it out of sight. That's all." He still couldn't believe that his friend would be foolish enough to pack a deadly weapon in the van.

"Yes, Mommy." Shaking his head impatiently, Jonathan sped up to pass a slow-moving sedan. "Brother," he grumbled to himself as he inspected the oncoming traffic, "you city girls."

Bucky fought back a retort. The damage was already done, he realized. *Just stay low-key*. There was obviously more to Jonathan than he had discovered in chemistry class. The oversized junior had a sinister side to him that was too unpredictable for Bucky's liking.

"Hey, we're getting hungry back here!" Tracy's voice broke through the rock music and Bucky's reverie.

"That ice cream wore off already?" Despite his smoldering anger, he tried to sound cheerful.

"Uh huh. Jill and I vote for some supper."

Jonathan glanced down at his watch and frowned. "Come on, you guys. We still got a long way to go.

We haven't even hit Oregon yet.''

Tracy gave an impatient little motion to Bucky, indicating that the music was too loud. Ignoring Jonathan, he reached up and eased down the volume.

''It takes just as much time to eat later as it does now,'' the little redhead pointed out. ''I mean, that's a scientific fact.''

In spite of himself Bucky laughed. ''She's got you there, Shultz.''

''Yeah, yeah, yeah.'' Jonathan wiped off a smudge over on Bucky's side of the windshield. ''Looks like some places to eat up there.''

Squealing the van over into the right-hand lane, he pulled off the freeway into a small complex of gas stations and fast-food restaurants. ''What do you guys want?''

''Well, not junk stuff,'' Jill declared. ''Let's go over there.'' She pointed toward a coffee shop.

The four young people climbed out of the van and stretched their limbs. ''It's getting cold,'' Tracy observed as she pulled on a sweater.

''Lock up, everybody.'' Jonathan fumbled awkwardly under the front seat as Bucky and the girls began walking toward the entrance to the restaurant.

''Hurry up.'' Bucky held open the door for the girls and turned to see what was delaying his friend. Carrying a tattered knapsack, the other boy puffed up to him.

''Sorry. Had to get my wallet.''

Inside the brightly-lit restaurant, Jonathan's good humor seemed to return. He was a clever guy, Bucky had to admit, as he listened to the back-and-forth bantering between the boy and Tracy. Sitting on the other side, Jill suppressed a smile as she slowly devoured a chocolate milkshake.

"Well, that's 975 more calories I'm going to have to work off," Tracy observed as she wiped away a stray fragment of pie.

"Are you kidding?" Bucky laughed. "You must weigh all of 98 pounds."

"And half of that's her brain." Jonathan snickered, his owlish eyes dancing.

"Oh, ha ha." Tracy picked up the bill. "Come on, you children. Everybody get out your money." Without a pause she rattled off each person's tab, including California tax and a one-fourth share of the tip.

Bucky pretended to sigh. "Maybe you're a little too smart," he grumbled.

The redhead snuggled closer to him and smirked. "Oh, you love it, and you know it."

The tall boy didn't answer, but he felt his heartbeat quicken. Despite Tracy's overpowering intellect, she still had a perky softness about her that was beginning to make him tingle. Sitting across from the couple, Jonathan's face suddenly seemed to reveal a trace of jealousy.

Jill heaved a big sigh as she began to dig through her purse. "We should have picked some richer guys to go out with, Tracy." She gave Jonathan a sarcastic little glare.

He looked at her, then over at Bucky and Tracy. "You want me to pick this up for everybody?" His voice had an edge to it as he looked down at the bill.

"Sure." Tracy laughed quietly as she nudged the slip of paper toward him.

He shifted casually in his seat. "Hey, I can get us out of here without paying at all."

Jill wrinkled up her nose. "What are you talking about?"

Reaching down under the table Jonathan pulled his knapsack free and began to tug on the zipper.

Bucky froze. A silent warning began to pound at his mind. *Watch it!* Without meaning to, he pulled away from Tracy and leaned across the table. "I . . ."

Jonathan licked his lips as he finished unzipping the bag. Glancing carefully around, he reached inside.

"Stop it!" Bucky blurted out the words without realizing what he was saying. Somehow the mysterious gleam in the other boy's eyes had given away what was about to happen.

Slowly pulling the pistol free, Jonathan set it on the table and looked from one to the other, as if daring them to say anything. Tracy gave an involuntary little gasp of shock, clutching at Bucky's shirt sleeve. "Oh my . . ."

"Here's our meal ticket, children." Jonathan looked defiantly at the three of them. "You all want to pay $23.60 or just walk out of here?"

A long, ominous silence hung in the air. The other three sat in wordless amazement, staring at the jet-black weapon.

"Put that away. Right now." Bucky tried to keep his voice even, but inside his heart was racing like an out-of-control jackhammer. "I mean it, man."

The red-haired boy gave him an impatient look. "I was just kidding." He glanced behind him toward the cash register. A lone clerk was accepting payment from another group of customers, but no one was within earshot.

Slipping the weapon back into the knapsack, he pulled the zipper tight. "Come on, let's get out of here."

Tracy hesitated for a moment, then shrugged. "Yeah." She looked over at Bucky as if to solicit moral support. "Let's go."

At the counter each of the four wordlessly paid a share of the tab. Accepting his change, Bucky held open the door for the girls. "Can you believe that?" he muttered so that only Tracy could hear. She rolled her eyes and grimaced, slipping her hand into the crook of his arm as they went back to the van.

Bucky pulled open the door to the passenger area and helped her in. "Just hang on a minute," he murmured, sliding the door back into place. He motioned with his head away from the van. "Get over here, Shultz. I gotta talk to you."

Sighing, Jonathan ambled over to where Bucky waited for him in the darkening shadows. "Now what?" His voice revealed his returning dourness.

Bucky took a breath. "Look . . ." He hesitated, eyeing the other boy. "No more with the guns. I'm not kidding."

Jonathan shuffled his feet impatiently. "Oh, that again?" he complained. "For heaven's sake, Stone! I was just playin' around."

"I don't care what you were doing," Bucky retorted, his voice rising. "No more, man."

"Oh, and says who?"

Bucky took a step forward. "I'm telling you to can it. You show that thing again and . . ." His mind raced. "I mean, once more and this trip is off. The girls and I . . ."

"It's a long walk home." Jonathan's voice was equally hard now.

A long angry pause rose between them. Nearby on the freeway Bucky could hear the *zip zip zip* of cars going by.

"Look, Shultz." Bucky tried to bring his temper under control. "I don't want to have a big battle with you. I mean, really. Let's just put the whole thing away and have a good weekend, man."

Jonathan said nothing, the knapsack still dangling from his left hand. At last he gave a little nod. "Yeah, OK."

The tension between the boys was still heavy as they climbed into the front of the van. Without a word Jonathan inserted the key and gunned the engine to life. Throwing the van into reverse, he wheeled out of the small parking lot and headed toward the expressway.

Bucky turned to see what the girls were doing. In the murky darkness he could read the curiosity written across Tracy's face. He gave Jill a wordless little motion with his head. Jonathan, staring down the highway, edged the van up toward 80 miles an hour again.

Trading places with the dark-haired girl, he slipped into the seat next to Tracy. "What was that all about?'' she murmured in a low voice. ''Sounded kind of lively from here.''

He shrugged. ''Nothing.''

She slipped closer to him. ''You boys and your little weapons.''

Without quite knowing why, he reached out and took her hand. The turmoil of the argument at the restaurant had left him shaken. He forced thoughts of Lisa from his mind for the moment. *I'll figure that out later!*

The next two hours went by without event. Conversation between the front and back seats was minimal, especially with the ever-present beat of the nearest pop station jarring through four speakers. However, Jonathan's resentment slowly began to melt and by the time the van pulled into a service station in Eugene, Oregon, he was joking with Jill again.

''At least gas is cheaper up here than at Hampton,'' he grumbled to Bucky, sounding his good-natured self.

''We gonna try to stay somewhere here tonight?''

Jonathan scratched his head. ''Yeah, I guess. It's gettin' late, and here's as good as Portland. If we get a decent start in the morning, we'll make it to the game no sweat.''

''Where shall we stay?''

Jonathan reached out and pulled the gas pump handle free, wincing as he noticed the tally on the pump. ''Cheap motel, I guess. I'll ask the cashier where's good.''

''Two rooms instead of one,'' Bucky observed. ''Even then, it's going to be more than I thought.''

"I know." Pulling his wallet out, Jonathan fished for a bill. "Can you help me with $10 here? Like I said, we'll get more when we get up to Seattle."

A few minutes later they wheeled out of the brightly lit station. "Lady said that about a mile ahead there's a couple of motels that aren't too bad. Past the second light."

In the back seat Bucky looked at Tracy. "Getting tired?"

"Uh huh." She put her head down on his shoulder again. "How about you?"

"Yeah, a little bit." The emotional strain of feuding with Jonathan had left him weary.

Up ahead a green light abruptly turned yellow. Shifting in the driver's seat, Jonathan hesitated, then punched the accelerator. The van shot forward, hurtling through the intersection and the glowing red light.

CHAPTER 8

CHASE!

A duffel bag perched on the van's interior storage unit tumbled to the floor as the van lurched down the street. "Take it easy, Shultz!" Bucky snapped, rubbing his ankle where the rough canvas bag had hit him. "That sucker was red all the way."

"Naah, it was still yellow."

"No way. That was red before you even hit the gas," Jill put in.

An eerie wail suddenly filled the air, sending a thrill of fear through Bucky. He jerked his head around and stared back through the dust-covered rear window. "Oh, no!" He twisted around on the seat to make sure. "Cops!"

In the driver's seat, Jonathan glanced anxiously in both mirrors. The red glow from the police cruiser reflected ominously into his eyes. Pounding in anger on the steering wheel, he muttered an epithet.

"I told you it was red," Bucky bit off the words, his voice rising.

"Shut up!" Looking into the mirror again, Jonathan smacked his right hand against the dashboard in anger. "Why me?"

"Well, pull over," Tracy said. "May as well get it over with."

"Shoot." Even from the back seat Bucky could see the red flush beginning to creep up Jonathan's neck. "Man, this is gonna cost me a bundle and a half."

"Well, just . . ." Bucky looked around as the siren wailed a second time. "Come on, pull over."

Easing his foot off the accelerator, Jonathan began to pull the van over to the side of the road. Far down the road loomed the flicker of a green light and a warning signal for a set of railroad tracks. As the van and police car slowed to a near-crawl a huge 18-wheeler began to rumble past them on the left.

Bucky could see two policemen in the patrol car, one of them speaking into the radió mike. The menacing red light still flickered in the Oregon darkness.

Suddenly he heard a squeal of tires as the van shot forward. The engine roared in protest as Jonathan abruptly punched the accelerator to the floor. Darting ahead at high speed, the van cut between the front of the semi and a row of parked cars, missing the huge truck by inches.

"What are you doing?" Bucky's startled shout cut through the renewed wail of the police car.

"I'm drivin', baby." Holding the gas pedal to the floor, Jonathan hurtled the van down the rough two-lane road, glancing frantically in the rearview mirror. The police cruiser, blocked momentarily by the parked cars, finally swung out from the other side of the slow-moving truck and began to give chase, but its glowing red lights were now several hundred yards behind them.

"You're crazy! Pull over!" Bucky and Tracy both began to shout incoherently at the driver. A desperate sense of foreboding seized Bucky as he remembered his friend's irrational behavior earlier at the restaurant. "Come on, Shultz! It's just a traffic ticket!"

Two hundred yards ahead of them the railroad warning lights suddenly began to *ding*. "There we go!" Jonathan muttered, a strange note of exultation in his voice. Off to the left a train engine with three flatbed cars behind it began to approach the crossing. The engine's whine grew as the van raced to beat the diesel locomotive to the intersection.

"Shultz! You'll never make it!" Pushing Tracy away, Bucky stumbled to the front of the van and tugged at Jonathan's sleeve. In the right-hand seat Jill sat paralyzed in white-faced anxiety.

"Shut up!" His face tight with determination, the heavy-set boy took one more glance in the rearview mirror. "Come on, baby." With one final burst of speed, the van shot across the railroad tracks a scant 40 feet in front of the train.

"Yeah!" Not letting up on the gas pedal, Jonathan glanced behind him again. The patrol car had squealed to an angry stop on the other side of the tracks.

"You're an idiot!" Angry beyond words now,

Bucky pounded his fist against the side of Jill's seat. "What's the matter with you, Shultz?"

His eyes still flashing, Jonathan turned his head for just a moment. "Are you forgetting about the gun we got sittin' in here with us?" He took a breath. "You think I wanna get stuck with that thing in my pocket?"

Bucky shook his head in angry disbelief. "They wouldn't have searched the van just for you runnin' a red light."

"Well, they would now."

"Those cops just went off to the left," Tracy announced, her voice still shaking. "Wait! There's a cross street down there. Here they come again! They're over there on that block."

Slamming his fist down on the steering wheel again, Jonathan bellowed another epithet. In the distance they could hear the familiar wail of the siren.

"Just stop! Stop right now," Bucky pleaded. "We keep going, it's just going to get worse."

"No way." Jonathan scanned the horizon. "Right up there we're downtown."

"So?" Jill spoke for the first time, her voice tight with fear.

"Just wait, babies." Jonathan spat out the last word as his eyes darted from side to side.

Still traveling at high speed the vehicle approached the edges of the business part of town. Almost 9:00 now, traffic was relatively light as they rushed past a photo shop and a cluster of convenience stores. One block away a yellow light flickered to red.

Jonathan didn't hesitate. Speeding up again he

roared through the intersection, narrowly missing a car going through the other way.

"Cut it out! You're going to kill us!" Bucky said. Off to the left and still well behind them, the patrol car was clearly visible now as it picked up speed. Jonathan accelerated to pass a slow-moving taxicab as the next intersection loomed ahead.

Abruptly the van squealed to a slow as it veered into the right lane, narrowly missing a motorcycle parked next to the curb. Just as the light turned red, Jonathan make a hard right turn, bouncing up over the curb as he maneuvered into the cross street and barreled down the road.

"What are you doing?" Jill, clutching at the door handle with both hands, jerked her gaze around in desperation.

"There ain't no place to run here," Jonathan snapped. "This place is empty! Where am I gonna go to get away?"

"Just pull over," Bucky pleaded once again. "Please, Jonathan!"

"Forget it!" Swerving sharply to the left, the van cut across the pathway of oncoming traffic at the next cross street and accelerated through a yellow light into the main road. The patrol car was now a bare four blocks back.

Muttering inaudibly to himself, Jonathan scanned both sides of the road. About three blocks ahead was a huge parking lot filled with cars. A blinking movie marquee announced the titles of four current features.

"There we go!" he said hoarsely as he pushed the gas pedal to the floor. Rumbling noisily down the street, the van veered to the right and into the parking lot just seconds before the police car pulled into view on the main road.

The shock absorbers on the van squealed in protest as the vehicle bounced painfully up and down on the lot entrance at high speed. Jonathan looked from left to right for an empty stall.

"There!" Jill, despite her fear, pointed out a spot.

"Yeah!" It was just next to one occupied by a second van. Whipping the wheel to the right, Jonathan lurched the vehicle to a stop and shut off the lights and engine. "Get down, you guys!"

Awkwardly pulling his ample frame into the small area of space between the driver's seat and the right-hand passenger area, Jonathan risked a peek out the window. The police car, traveling slower now, was just going past the theater parking lot.

"I think we ditched 'em!" Pumping his fist in exultation, he looked over at Jill, who was huddled against the door, exhausted fear on her face. "Them suckers just went right by."

"This is the worst . . ." From the back seat, Tracy's voice trailed off. She looked up at Bucky, who was still on the seat in an upright position.

"Man, Stone, what is the matter with you? I said to get down!" Jonathan bristled.

"No." Bucky remained where he was, his heart-beat slowly returning to normal. He stared evenly at the stocky driver, his temper barely in control.

"Are you crazy?"

Bucky licked his lips. "Somebody else's going to

have to decide who's crazy around here. But I ain't moving."

Jonathan growled another curse to himself as he raised up to glance out the window again. "All quiet out there. Man, I wonder if we really did get away with it."

"I'm sure they got your license plate," Jill retorted, still in her crouched position.

"That's right." Bucky had to struggle to choke back his anger.

"I don't know." Jonathan avoided his friend's smoldering gaze and addressed himself to the two girls. "We were just about stopped, an' maybe they hadn't written it down yet."

Tracy heaved a sarcastic little sigh. "Whoopie. So what are we gonna do?"

Jonathan twisted around and climbed into the area between the front and back seats. "We sit tight until the movie gets out," he told them. "Then when these two hundred cars head out, we roll right out with 'em."

HIDING OUT IN THE PARKING LOT

The minutes passed by in silence. A sick feeling washing over him, Bucky fully expected any minute to hear the harsh staccato of a police loudspeaker interrupt the uneasy quiet.

"No kidding, this is the dumbest thing I've ever gotten into," he muttered to Tracy. She responded with a blank, fatigued look.

One of the movie features let out, but only a few patrons headed for their cars. The streets lining the huge parking lot were nearly deserted now, illuminated by the fuzzy orange glow of the street lights.

"How long are we going to sit here?" Jill asked.

Jonathan didn't answer for a moment, his owlish face a study in frustration. At last he glanced at his watch. "Seems to me like most of these cars are probably here to see that big Cruise film. So when ιey head out, we'll go too."

"Then what?" Tracy wanted to know.

The stocky junior shrugged. "I dunno. Maybe we should just go straight to the freeway and bomb out of here. Get to Portland quick."

Bucky wet his lips, wanting to speak but not wishing to further antagonize him. "Boy, I don't know . . ."

"What?" Jonathan's retort revealed his lingering irritation.

Taking a breath, Bucky said, "Look, man, I still think we ought to, you know, give it up." His voice betrayed uncertainty.

"What?"

"Look, we ran a red light and then panicked. But nobody's hurt, we didn't run over anybody. Why don't we just . . ."

"Drive up to police headquarters and say, 'We give up'? You want to *surrender*?"

Bucky nodded. "Why not?"

"Oh, for heaven's sake!" Jonathan half-raised himself to a sitting position and glared at Bucky. "First off, it ain't you who ran a red light or zoomed through town on a cops-and-robbers ride. It ain't you with a gun in the glove box. Sounds like you're just real happy to sell *me* out."

"We'll all do it together," Bucky said.

"Oh, right." Jonathan shook his head. "Look, the cops pull somebody over, he gets away on a lucky fluke like we did, those guys just shrug and say, 'Well, goody for him. We'll get the next fool who rolls into town.' I'll bet those cops are already home in bed."

"Then what are we sitting here sweating for?" Bucky retorted.

"Just insurance." Jonathan rubbed at something in his eyes, which were starting to redden with the strain. "I want to make sure they get good and bored and sleepy before we pull out."

Tracy abruptly pulled on her jacket. "Well, I'm gonna go find out when that movie ends. If I sit in here any longer, I'm going to puke."

"I'm going with you." Bucky gave Jonathan a long look before reaching for his own jacket.

"I . . ." For a moment Jonathan seemed to want to protest. Sitting up in the van, he scanned the area around the parking lot, but the entire town of Eugene seemed to have gone to bed. "Shoot, I guess it don't matter. Nobody's going to know who you are or anything. Go ahead."

"Thanks." Bucky didn't try to mask his sarcasm. Opening the sliding door, he let Tracy out and then stepped out into the cold April air. Little gusts of vapor appeared with every breath as he wordlessly slid the door closed.

Tracy took his hand as they walked toward the theater entrance where a single employee sat inside the ticket booth. "Whooh, what a night," she muttered.

"What do you think?" Bucky shivered inside the thin jacket. "Think he's going to get away with it?"

"Probably," Tracy scowled. "He's probably right. Cops just figure, 'Oh, well.' "

"I don't know," he observed with a wince. "Seems to me after chasing some nut all through town like that, they take it kind of personal." He paused. "I just hope whatever happens, the rest of us don't get stuck."

The little redhead nodded. "Uh huh. One van, four jail cells."

Bucky felt a fresh stab of fear. Should he call the police himself and try to explain? He pushed the thought away.

When they reached the ticket window, the attendant cocked her head at the pair. Examining the sign, Bucky noticed that one film had a final 10:30 showing. He shook his head as the girl made a motion as if to ask them what they wanted.

"11:40. That's when that other film gets out." Bucky pointed. "But that animated feature ends in 20 minutes. Maybe some of these cars are here for that one."

"Yeah." Tracy's hand tightened in his. "You want to walk around a little bit?"

"OK." The couple did a long tour around the far edge of the parking lot, wordlessly avoiding the litter of soda cups and candy wrappers. Bucky's mind was a jumbled blur of Lisa, his precarious situation, and the girl who was now clutching his hand in thoughtful silence.

"Whatcha thinking about?" she abruptly asked, her voice low.

He hesitated. "Just worried about all this stuff."

"It'll be OK," she shrugged.

Bucky nodded slowly. "Yeah, maybe." He thought for a moment as they began the slow walk back to the van. "But, you know, for me . . ." He paused. "Being a Christian and everything, I . . ."

Tracy waited expectantly. "I mean, just getting away with it isn't the big thing. I want to do what's right for God."

Tracy digested his words. "You weren't driving." She cocked an eyebrow at him.

"Yeah, but . . ." The thoughts deep within his mind threatened to push their way to the surface. Being on a guy-girl trip when his parents thought he was with three other guys . . . juggling romance with both Lisa and this little redhead. It was more than he could even think about, let alone try to explain.

They climbed back into the van and told the others when the various films ended. "If very many people come out after this Disney film, maybe we could go then," Tracy concluded. "Otherwise we gotta wait here another whole hour."

Jonathan nodded, his resentment somewhat cooled. "Yeah, we'll see."

The next ten minutes passed by in fitful silence. At last a number of patrons exited and began walking to their cars. The low rumble of post-movie conversations filtered in through the windows of the Chevy van.

"What do you think?" Bucky asked.

Jonathan nodded. "Looks like about half the place is going right now. Guess this is as good a chance as any."

"Are you going to head to the freeway?" Jill asked.

"I don't know." Jonathan climbed back into the driver's seat. "Play it by ear."

A moment later a tall teenager and his girlfriend

climbed into the van right next to Jonathan's. "Here we go, you guys." Jonathan revved his engine and pulled into line right behind the other van. A string of about six cars began to slowly make its way down the street where a string of frosty green traffic lights beckoned.

They drove several blocks hiding in the relative anonymity of the little string of cars. At the last light, two cars continued to go straight, but the car in front of Jonathan slowly turned to the right. After a moment's hesitation he followed, staying a careful distance behind the other car.

"Now what?" Tracy asked.

"Just hang on." Jonathan swiped impatiently at a thin sheen of fog that was beginning to build up on the windshield. "Hey, there's a motel down here."

"You want to just stop?"

Jonathan slowed to a crawl as they passed the small lodging establishment. "Yeah, maybe." He turned to face the others. "The freeway's clear on the other side of town, and we're still a long ways from Portland." A moment later he appeared to make up his mind.

"This is it, then?" Bucky asked.

"Yeah." He drove a block further down the road as if looking for a place to turn around. But a moment later he wheeled carefully to the left and down a small side street. Several old vehicles lined it.

"What are you doing?" Bucky wondered.

"Gonna park here. Just in case."

Bucky was too weary to argue with his friend's logic any longer. Jonathan eased the big van into position between two sagging station wagons and turned off the key. For a moment the boy sat in the darkness, thinking.

"Let's go then." Tracy picked up her small duffel bag and moved toward the door.

Locking the van carefully, Jonathan followed the others toward the motel. As they got closer he fell into step beside Bucky. "Maybe you better do the talking here. Just in case . . ." His voice trailed off. "I can wait outside."

Bucky shrugged. "Whatever."

Even now the other boy couldn't resist a little jab. "What do you guys say? Just one room? Really make it a party night?"

All three students turned and glared at him. "Enough party already," Tracy snapped.

"I know. I know. Just kidding." Jonathan shook his head defensively and muttered something inaudible to himself. "Go for it, Stone."

Bucky and Tracy pulled open the door and entered the small motel lobby. A sleepy-looking woman in her early 50s set down a novel and peered out at them. "What do you kids want?"

He gulped. "Do you have any rooms?"

"Uh huh." She shoved a registration pad at him. "Just the two of you?"

He flushed as he shook his head. "No, there are four of us." He looked at Tracy. "We need two rooms. One for my friend and me and one for the girls."

The lady shrugged. "Where are the others?"

"Outside." Bucky picked up the pen. "They're kind of tired."

The matron gave him a disinterested look. "You can just fill it out for everybody."

He hesitated over the form. Right below the address line was a box asking for make of car and license number. Leaving it blank he slid the card back to the clerk.

"$23.00 a night including tax. For each room. Payment up front."

Without a word Tracy opened her purse and handed Bucky a $20 bill. He shot her a grateful look. Adding it to his own depleted little pile, he handed over the cash and accepted the two keys.

"Checkout's at ten," the woman grunted, returning to her book.

Outside Bucky handed one of the room keys to Tracy. "Here we are, Shultz." He forced a tight smile. "Hope you don't snore." The long, ugly evening had erected a barrier between the two boys that was impossible to miss.

CHAPTER 10

MIDNIGHT PRAYERS

Bucky stood in the shower, trying to soak in some much-needed warmth from the inadequate spray. Even the relaxing moments of isolation in the tiny bathroom didn't wash away the prickly feeling that lingered between the two boys.

"Come on, man." Jonathan's voice penetrated the thin bathroom door. "Give me a turn in there."

Bucky let the shower go on for another few moments before reluctantly turning off the water. Reaching for a towel, he dried himself off and stepped out into the room. About all it contained were two double beds and a small chest of drawers.

Clad just in a pair of boxer shorts, Jonathan was idly flipping through the channels on the scruffy-looking television. "Giants got beat again," he shrugged.

Picking up some of his clothes, Bucky shoved them into the bottom drawer. *Lord, help me to get along with him.* "Shower's all yours."

Jonathan squeezed into the bathroom and shut the door.

Sinking down onto the bed closest to the door, Bucky closed his eyes with a fatigued sigh. The harrowing escape from the police earlier that evening and the sense of still-present danger had put a tight knot in his stomach that wouldn't go away. The quiet but insistent blare of the TV, masked by the sounds of running water, filled the cramped motel room, but he didn't hear it.

His mind replayed the convulsive events of the evening, lurching from scene to scene. The squeal of the van's tires during the chase was still fresh in his memory.

Forcing himself to think in methodical precision, he weighed the situation. Was it wrong to stand aside while Jonathan pulled off an escape from the police? Was Bucky's own silence actually helping his friend break the law? Or were the patrolmen already home in bed, having shrugged off the chase through town as just another punk who got away?

After what seemed like an hour, the running water in the next room slowed to a trickle. Jonathan emerged from the bathroom with his hair awry and water still dripping into his eyes. "Pretty lousy shower," he grumped.

Then he slipped on a pair of tattered pajamas and turned the TV knob to another channel. Glancing briefly at the commercial, he turned and faced Bucky. "Listen, man . . ."

Bucky waited, his face emotionless.

"I, uh . . . I'm sorry how all this turned out. You know, with the cops and all."

After a moment's pause, Bucky forced a nod. "OK."

"And the gun." Jonathan shrugged. "I guess it was kind of dumb. I mean, look at what it got me into. But having it around made me feel good."

Bucky looked directly at the other boy. "What are you going to do now?"

"What do you mean?"

"About the cops and everything."

Jonathan scratched at his still-damp head. "I don't get it, Stone. What are you driving at? You still want me to . . . what? Drive over to the precinct office and turn us all in? Four hours after the whole thing's over?" He gave a little snort. "Shucks, back at Hampton I've run through stop signs and stuff a hundred times. You want me to go in when we get back home and tell 'em, 'Well, hey, my conscience has been bothering me. Please charge me a couple of million bucks in back fines so I can sleep easier at night'? I mean, get real, Stone."

Bucky sat up and put his feet down on the floor, looking directly at his friend. "I don't know if that's what you should do. I admit it sounds dumb." He took a breath. "All I know is this: for us to run away from the cops like that was wrong. Stupid and wrong. Whether we got away with it or not, that's what I've got to live with."

"It ain't your problem, man."

The taller boy shook his head. "Look, Shultz." He tried to keep his voice calm. "You know I'm a

Christian. So I'm kind of dealing with a whole different set of rules. And in my . . . religion, getting away
with it isn't the point at all. As far as God's concerned,
we didn't get away with it at all."

A strange look crossed Jonathan's face. "You're
serious, aren't you?"

Bucky nodded. "Yeah. I feel real . . . I don't
know." He cocked his head to one side, looking at
him. "You know what I mean?"

"I guess. Kind of, anyway." Jonathan wadded up
his towel and tossed it on the floor. "But look. Like I
said, it's not your problem. You told me to stop, and
I didn't. Just forget about it and go to sleep."

Reaching over, Bucky brushed a piece of lint off
the thin bedspread. "I guess . . . things just haven't
turned out like I thought," he managed at last.

The other boy gave a little *humph*. "Oh, looked to
me like in at least one way, things were turnin' out
pretty good for you."

"What do you mean?"

"Miss Tracy Givenchy was all over you, my
friend." Jonathan gestured with his head toward the
adjacent room. "If you'd pushed your luck at all,
you'd be rooming with her right now. Which
wouldn't have bothered me at all." He grinned,
thinking about Jill.

Bucky's mind raced, trying to think of a response.
But his own thoughts about Tracy . . . and Lisa . . . and
about a Christian guy's integrity were too difficult to
even sort out, let alone explain to someone like
Jonathan Shultz. He let the remark pass.

It was midnight before Jonathan flipped the lights off

in the sparse motel room. He mumbled some one-sided conversation for a few moments, but finally lapsed into silence, giving Bucky an opportunity to pray.

Silently pouring out his thoughts to God, Bucky asked for wisdom to face the rest of the trip. "I don't know what I should have done, Lord," he confessed. "I mean, I didn't know any of this was going to happen. Please help me to think things through better next time." He prayed for Jonathan for several minutes, then asked God to show him a way to share Christ with his friend.

Even with the fatigue of the long freeway trip, it was hard to get to sleep. He kept remembering the jolt of that first moment when he climbed into the van and saw Tracy seated there. Miss Tracy Givenchy, the smartest girl he'd ever met. And one of the prettiest. Not a Christian, but with that little laugh and her evocative little glances.

Shifted uneasily in the lumpy bed, he then thought of Lisa. A disquieting sense began to creep over him that perhaps he was a little too easily swept off his feet by a girl's looks, regardless of her character values. Was it disloyal, even wrong, to entertain an interest in someone like Tracy at the very moment that Lisa was expectantly waiting up in Seattle? And Lisa—she shared his religious interests, but she did not yet share his Adventist heritage.

His mind went back to his sophomore year and the painful romance with Deirdre. Not a Christian either. After several dates and the realization that Bucky-and-Deirdre was a dead-end street, he had forced himself to break off the friendship. Now here

was Tracy. Napping next to him in the van with her
head on his shoulder and holding hands while they
walked through the parking lot. Was he playing out
the same failed scenario for a second year in a row?

It was so easy, he realized now, to simply shrug
when faced with a tough choice. To put off any
confrontation. Tracy or Lisa? *Can't think about it now.*
Two girls instead of two guys on the Baseball Weekend? *Oh well. What a surprise.* A date with Deirdre?
Why not? Deal with the consequences later.

The little digital clock on the dresser was almost at
1:00 a.m. when a quiet conviction began to settle
over him. Never again would he allow himself to
become involved with a girl who wasn't a Christian.
Not Tracy or Deirdre or anyone.

How his decision would change the weekend that
still loomed ahead, he had no way of telling. Romantic
candles had already been lit in Tracy's mind—he was
sure of that. And the little redhead had a hold on him
that would be hard to shake. But somehow God would
give him a way to extricate himself from a situation that
was bound to harm his relationship with Jesus.

At last he fell asleep.

The theme music of ESPN's morning baseball
report filtered through his consciousness in the morning. Jonathan, already dressed, gave Bucky's mattress
a kick. "Come on, Stone, we got a long drive still.
Ready to see our A's stomp all over those poor
Mariners?"

"For sure." Determined to bury yesterday's dis-
agreements, Bucky climbed out of bed. "Just give me
a second."

"I figure we better eat in the van. Get some more food when we get to the Kingdome."

It took Bucky just a few moments to wash and dress. Pausing for a moment in the solitude of the bathroom to pray, he asked God to give him strength in following through with his decisions of the night before.

When they knocked on the girls' door, it was Tracy who answered. "Oh, come on, you guys. It's too early." Still barefoot, she was wearing a tattered T-shirt, her tousled red hair drooping down into her eyes. She gave Bucky a sleepy little grin.

He gulped. *Lord, how am I ever going to go through with this?*

"Well, hurry up," Jonathan teased. "You need any help getting dressed?"

She wrinkled up her nose at both of them and slammed the door. Bucky laughed in spite of himself. "Guess she told you."

It was a good 15 minutes before the two girls finally came out. Tracy was carrying her tote bag and a big pillow with pictures of teddy bears all over it.

"What, your room didn't have pillows?" Bucky asked.

"Not with my little Pooh Bear on it," she sniffed.

"Let me help you carry some of that."

She handed him her tote bag as they headed down the street toward the van. "You sleep all right?"

"Yeah, not bad." He looked down at her. "How 'bout you?"

"Oh, Jill wanted to watch some old Clint Eastwood show that came on. But I fell asleep."

Jonathan unlocked the van and the four students

piled all the gear into the cargo area. "Here we go again," Jill observed, climbing herself up into the front passenger seat. She pulled down the sun visor and peered into the mirror, dabbing at her makeup.

Bucky shifted some of the bags on the floor to make room for his long legs. Easing himself into the bench seat next to Tracy, he tried to cover up a yawn.

"You said you slept good," Tracy laughed.

"I guess not good enough."

She gave him a sly look. "Dreaming real hard about me, I hope." ·

He gulped.

Fumbling with the keys, Jonathan finally turned on the ignition. With a sputter, the engine rumbled to life.

All at once a long black-and-white car came careening around the corner. Squealing to a stop right in front of the van, two officers jumped out.

"What in the world?" Jonathan whirled around in his seat. Behind the van, a second patrol car had just pulled into position, blocking them from backing out. Two more officers slowly approached the van from the rear, hands on their holsters.

"Oh my . . ." Tracy, her face white with panic, looked from one boy to the other. "What's going on?"

"Get out of the van with your hands up." The staccato voice reverberated off the walls of the apartment buildings lining the quiet street as a fifth officer, his body shielded by the open door of the lead patrol car, spoke through a megaphone. "You're under arrest."

CHAPTER 11

BUSTED

The pounding in Bucky's chest was so real he felt like he was going to faint. The red lights flashed directly into his eyes and made him dizzy.

"Oh, man!" Jonathan looked straight ahead, his pudgy face pale and perspiring. "We are dead meat!"

"Please exit the vehicle. Slowly." The harsh amplified voice punctuated the air again.

His limbs weak, Bucky edged toward the door. It required several tries to undo the latch and slide the door free. Taking a deep breath, he tried to stop his hands from shaking.

"Slowly!" The words crackled in the students' ears. "Keep your hands where we can see them."

Climbing out, Bucky carefully stepped away from the van and onto the sidewalk. Tracy followed a moment later, her lips quivering slightly.

The next few minutes were an agonizing blur as the patrolmen lined up the four students against the side of the van. Bucky listened dully to the recitation of Miranda rights. "Anything you say can and will be used against you in a court of law . . ." He glanced over at Jill, who was almost in tears.

One of the police officers set down the radio microphone and walked over to Jonathan. "We're not going to cuff you kids," he said, his tone curt, "but I want you to get in the back of the patrol cars. Without any fuss. You and you over here." He nodded toward Bucky and Tracy. "The two of you in this one."

His heart in his throat, Bucky climbed into the back seat of the black-and-white sheriff's car. Heavy metal mesh separated the pair from the driver up front. He leaned back against the cold fabric of the seat.

"I never thought this would happen," he muttered to Tracy, his voice shaking just a little bit. "After last night, I mean. I figured Jonathan was right."

"What do we do?" Tracy pulled a tissue out of her pocket and dabbed at her nose.

"Just tell them exactly what happened." He looked over at the door, which had no inside handle. "Right down the line. Just tell them the truth."

It was a short drive to the Eugene police station on Pearl. The two officers in the front seat remained silent, one of them bent over a duty report, filling in the information with a black pen. The radio squawked instructions once, but the two men answered in monosyllables.

"Everybody out." The driver pulled into a marked slot in the station parking lot and shut off the engine. Two other policemen pulled open the passenger doors and waited for Bucky and Tracy to climb out. Already standing at the entrance to the two-story building, Jonathan and Jill were accompanied by two other armed guards.

Bucky looked behind him as the Chevy van pulled into view. The policeman driving the maroon vehicle wheeled into the parking lot and positioned it well away from the other cars.

"Let's go." Motioning the four young people into the building, the men led them down the hallway and into a room with a long table lined with chairs. "Everybody sit down, but no talking."

Bucky sank into one of the folding metal chairs and glanced over at Jonathan. The expression on the stocky junior's face was difficult to interpret. He glanced at Bucky and shook his head as if to admit his error.

A short Asian officer stepped into the room. "I need ID from all of you if you've got it," he said. "Driver's licenses, school ID, whatever."

Bucky reached into his back pocket and pulled out his wallet. Slipping his license free he handed it wordlessly to the officer, who collected them from all four students. A moment later he came over to Bucky.

"Mr. Stone, I'm going to ask you to go with Officer Shelton to Room A6 down the hall. He'll take your statement there. Miss Givenchy, we need you to go with Mr. Orland here. The two of you just wait here for a moment."

Numbly Bucky rose and followed the police officer down the hall. "In here, Stone." The man pulled the door open and motioned inside. "Let's see what this is all about."

Sitting down across from Bucky he pulled a thick pad out of the top drawer and looked across at the young student. "You've been advised of your rights. Are you willing to talk to me?"

Bucky nodded without speaking.

"Now, we've got you people involved last evening in a traffic-light violation and then an evasion of arrest along around 9:00, more or less." He made a notation on the chart. "Two of our men took down license plate and description out at the railroad crossing, then tracked you into town at extremely high speeds, at least two more red-light violations, four or five reckless-driving situations, and then some-how you kids got away from us." He gave Bucky a pointed look. "But now here we are. Have I about got it right?"

Bucky gulped. "Yes, sir."

The officer nodded. "OK. That's good for starters. Why don't we begin with who was driving?" His pen was poised over the pad.

"Jonathan." Bucky hesitated just a moment before answering. "It's his van. He drove the whole way."

"Including during the chase and everything?"

"Yes, sir."

The man paused for a moment. "Did you try to get him to stop?"

"About a hundred times."

"But he just kept going?"

Bucky nodded.

The officer asked him several questions about his

home address and personal information, dutifully recording the answers without comment. Finally he looked up again. "You been friends with Shultz long?"

"No, just this semester. We're lab partners."

Another pause. "And he drove the whole way, you say?"

"Yeah."

The man set down his clipboard and looked at him. "Let me just tell you something here for your own good. Now maybe it was Shultz driving and maybe it wasn't. We'll get statements from all four of you. But think about this: anything you want to tell me, right now's the time to do it. Any part of somebody's story needs changing, you can do it right now. Without penalty, so to speak. Later on things won't be nearly so cheerful if I find out things didn't happen exactly like you said." His voice was even, but his eyes bore holes through Bucky.

The student gulped. "I'm telling you the truth."

"Just so we understand each other."

Someone knocked on the door. "Come in," the policeman called out.

A younger officer came in and handed a handwritten note to Shelton. He raised an eyebrow and cast a glance at Bucky before handing the slip of paper back. "Thanks," he murmured. Bucky watched as the door closed behind the departing officer.

"Well, I guess we've got one more little bit of trivia to explore," the man continued. "Has to do with a pretty hefty weapon found in your van. Fully loaded automatic. Know anything about it?"

A fresh wave of fear hit Bucky in the gut.

"That's Jonathan's too," he managed, sensing how lame his responses must sound. "He kind of collects them as a hobby. Or at least his folks do."

"He brought it?"

"Uh huh."

"Did you know he had it along? Concealed in the car?"

"No, sir. Not until we were already on the road." He swallowed hard. "We already had kind of a fight over it. Back last night." Without fanfare he described the scene in the restaurant.

"But the gun was his? You didn't even handle it or anything?"

"No, sir."

The policeman's face didn't reveal any clues about his thoughts. "Well, Mr. Stone, we're going to see how all these stories line up, you understand. And we're going to ask you to let us fingerprint you. That's just for starters." He rose to his feet, towering over him. "Please wait here."

The minutes dragged by in painful silence. Against the far wall an old clock without a second hand ticked its way toward 11:00. He breathed a prayer for the other three students. Jonathan, especially, was in serious trouble, he realized. Bucky had a deepening sense of foreboding that he was too.

More than half an hour passed before the same officer returned. "Mr. Stone, would you come with me, please?"

Bucky followed the policeman to a room in the back of the station where a female clerk carefully took ink prints of his fingers. Each swirly black stain on the white police report seemed a fresh reminder of his poor judgment.

"Thank you, Mr. Stone," the woman said when she had finished. "You can wipe your fingers off with this." She handed him a chemically moistened paper towel.

Several minutes later a policewoman ushered Tracy and Jill into the same room. "You folks can stay here for now," she announced before she stepped back out into the hallway.

Bucky looked over at Tracy, not knowing whether or not they were allowed to speak to each other. He glanced around to see if there was anyone to ask, but the room was empty. "Are you guys OK?"

Jill nodded. The eyes of both girls looked red from crying.

"What did they ask you?"

"Everything," Tracy answered. "Who was driving, whose van, the works."

"What did you tell them?" He looked over at Jill.

"Told them the truth. What else?" The dark-haired girl shrugged.

A flicker of hope penetrated Bucky's bleak mood. With three of them giving the same testimony, maybe they could soon extricate themselves from the jam. He breathed another prayer for Jonathan.

At 1:00 the policewoman returned and went right to her desk without addressing the three students.

Several times Bucky found himself glancing at the clock. Today's ballgame was obviously going to happen without them, he realized. A moment later he sensed the incongruity of worrying about missing a game after the mess they were in.

Collecting his courage, he finally went over to the officer. "Excuse me, ma'am?"

She looked up at him, peering over her glasses. "Yes?"

"Is it OK if . . . I mean, are we allowed to make phone calls?"

She nodded. "Yes, I think it's all right now." She pointed out the door. "Pay phone's right there."

Going out to the hall telephone, he dialed the Nichols' home in Seattle and carefully entered his family's credit card number.

Lisa answered on the first ring. "Hi!" He could hear the sound of her stereo in the background. "I didn't think you'd call me from the ballpark. When are you going to come over and see me?"

Her enthusiasm made him wince. "Listen, I'm afraid . . ." He fought back the feelings of frustration that threatened to twist at his insides again. "We're in a lot of trouble down here."

"Where? Bucky, what is it?"

Keeping his voice low he described the dilemma, trying to keep it brief.

"Oh, no." She groaned. "How could you guys be so dumb?"

"Boy, I don't know."

"Well, what's going to happen?"

"I don't know," he repeated. "They've had Jonathan off by himself for a couple of hours. So I've got no idea what's happening."

After a long silence, she said, "I guess all you can

do is call me when you finally get out of there." Her voice sounded like she was trying to force herself to be casual. "I just hope it's not 20 years."

His stomach lurched. "I know."

Another pause. "Good luck, I guess."

"Yeah. I'll call you as soon as I can."

He returned to the room and sat down, staring at his shoes. Tracy leaned over and held onto his arm. "Hang in there, honey."

"Mr. Stone?"

His head jerked up. Officer Shelton, his face still an emotionless mask, stood in the doorway. "Just a few more questions, if you don't mind."

"Sure." Giving Tracy a shrug, he followed Shelton down the hallway to the same room.

The man sat down without fanfare and looked over at the young student. "We did find Shultz's fingerprints all over the gun," he announced without fanfare. "And traces of yours as well."

CHAPTER 12

A DECENT
REPUTATION

Bucky's head spun. "Wha . . . what did you say?"

"Your fingerprints. Right there on the gun along with Jonathan's."

The man sat down and stared right through him. "What do you have to say about that?"

"I . . . I don't know what to say." The words came out weakly. "I just . . . I didn't touch it. I swear." He tried hard to think. "He had it in the glove compartment and then in his knapsack in the restaurant. But I never had it."

The man said nothing as he eyed him.

"Please. You've got to believe me." Now completely confused, Bucky didn't know what else he could say.

Officer Shelton sat for a moment without responding. At last, chewing on his lower lip with a questioning expression still on his face, he rose and went over to the other side of the room. Punching in a four-digit extension, he spoke in a low voice, covering the receiver so that Bucky couldn't listen in.

"Yeah, you're right," Bucky heard him say at last. "Until we find that out, nobody moves."

Hanging up the phone, he returned to Bucky. "Well, we're not getting very far. You and the girls all say it was Jonathan driving. But . . ."

"Well, what does he say?"

The man shrugged. "Not much. Frankly, we haven't gotten much of a story out of Mr. Shultz. The van's his, of course. Paperwork shows that. And he admits the gun's his too. Which he knows would be easy enough to prove. But on the rest—him driving during the getaway and all—he won't admit or deny nothin'. That's why we're still sitting here."

"So now what?"

The police officer shifted in his seat, studying him before responding. "Well, Mr. Stone, we're just kind of in a holding pattern. The way that van was goin' 80 through town, we figure it was either you or Shultz driving and not that little redhead. Probably Shultz, although the girls might be covering for you. I don't know. Gun's got fingerprints of both you boys. So here we sit."

Lord, please help me! Bucky breathed another silent prayer.

"Is it OK if I call my folks?"

A nod. "All right." The man motioned toward the regular office phone on his desk. "Credit card?"

"Yeah."

Shelton punched in a 9 and then handed the receiver to Bucky, making no move to excuse himself.

Bucky dialed in the number of his dad's office and entered the necessary digits again. A receptionist answered. "Hampton Mortgage."

"Is Mr. Stone in?"

A pause. "He's on another line. May I help you?"

"This is Bucky. His son." He drew a deep breath. "I'm in kind of an emergency. Any chance you can get him?"

"Let me try." Some "hold" music came on the line for a moment before the receiver crackled.

"Bucky? Is that you?"

The familiar voice on the other end caused a brief stirring of emotion in Bucky. "Yeah, Dad."

"What's wrong?"

For the second time Bucky explained the crisis. "Oh, boy." A brief silence. "You guys are in a mess." Dad's mutter held no trace of anger.

"What can we do?"

"I can fly up there right now if I need to," Dad said. "Take a couple of hours to get a flight to Eugene, but I'll be happy to come."

"I don't know," his son stammered. "I mean, we didn't do anything. It was all Jonathan."

"Well, sure, I know," Dad responded. "But you can understand how it looks to them." His voice seemed puzzled. "But that business with the gun. You're sure you didn't have anything to do with it?"

"Dad, I'm positive."

"Wait a minute." Bucky could hear his father whispering something to one of the secretaries.

"Yeah, United. Let me know."

Mr. Stone came back on. "Didn't you tell me you and this Jonathan spent an evening doing some target shooting over at his place? When you went over there to pick up some school books or something?"

It was as if a thunderbolt had struck Bucky. "That's right!" Suddenly his breath began to come in excited little gasps. "How could I have been so stupid to forget that?"

Covering the receiver with his hand, he turned excitedly to the officer. "My dad just reminded me that a couple weeks ago I was over at Jonathan's, and we shot some tin cans off the porch. With that same gun." He spoke into the receiver again. "Hang on, Dad."

The man shrugged slightly. "Pretty convenient story," he responded with a hint of cynicism in his voice.

"No way! It's my dad. You can ask him yourself!"

Officer Shelton shook his head. "We'll check it out," he said. "But I'm not here to get a testimonial from your dad."

The sudden euphoria began to fade. *Why wouldn't they believe him?* He returned to the phone. "Dad, let me call you back as soon as I can."

"You want me to come up?"

Bucky took a breath. "No, not yet. Let me call you first."

"All right, son. I'll either be right here or at the house. I won't go any place else until I hear from you."

"Thanks."

Replacing the receiver, Bucky turned around, but the officer had left the room. "Oh, boy," he muttered to himself, not knowing what to think. Would Jonathan corroborate the story of the target practice back at Hampton Beach? And why wasn't he telling the police he had been doing the driving?

Fifteen agonizing minutes went by. Impatiently Bucky watched as the clock hands slowly edged toward 2:00. Finally the officer returned. "Mr. Stone, why don't you follow me?"

His stomach still queasy with uneasiness, Bucky followed the patrolman down the hallway toward a small conference room. Jonathan sat with two other officers, and someone pointed Bucky to a seat.

"Now, look, men," Shelton said. "I really hope we can work this out. Shultz, here, isn't talking, and until we get our stories straight, I guess we can just sit here looking at each other."

Bucky glanced over at his friend. "What's going on?" he managed.

"Nothing." The other boy's gaze carried a warning. "I just don't think we should talk to them here until we have some kind of, you know, legal advice."

After staring at his shoes for a moment, Bucky said, "I guess you know I already answered their questions."

"Yeah, I figured that out." The stocky junior shrugged. "You can say what you want, but I'm not getting into it until I hear from my folks."

"When's that going to be?"

Jonathan shook his head. "Can't get hold of them. Tonight when they get home, I hope."

"So we're just going to sit here?"

"That's right, Stone," Jonathan said after an angry silence. "We're just going to sit here. *I'm* not going to go making up a whole bunch of stuff just so I can get out of here."

The last remark caught Bucky by complete surprise. "What . . . what are you talking about?"

"Nothing. Just shut up."

Over in the doorway Bucky could see two officers engaged in a quiet conversation. All at once the tension of the long day in police custody, combined with the frustration of Jonathan's stoic silence, brought a sickening flutter to his stomach. "I got to . . . where's the restroom?" he managed.

Officer Shelton shot him a sympathetic look. "Down the hall, second on the left."

"OK if I go?"

"Yeah."

For several long minutes Bucky remained in the restroom, waiting for his twisted insides to untie themselves. The emptiness in his stomach was partly to blame for his discomfort, he realized. He lingered as long as he dared before splashing his face with cold water and returning to the room where Jonathan and the trio of officers still waited. Bucky noticed that Jill and Tracy had now been brought into the same holding area. Tracy looked over at him without speaking.

He sat next to her. "We're missing the game," he said, trying to force a grin.

She nodded, edging closer to him. "Looks like a little worse than that."

Bucky noticed one of the men eyeing him. With a start, he realized how things might look to the law enforcement officers. Would they think she had been covering for him all morning?

"Bucky? Bucky Stone?" Again he glanced toward the doorway. A large man in his early 60s with silver-white hair was looking at him.

"Yes?"

"Would you come with me, please?"

Bucky felt the same little twitch of nerves as he rose to his feet and followed the officer upstairs. A large mahogany door had a sign on it: "Chief Gerald Norris."

The man motioned him inside. "Sit down, Stone."

Bucky obeyed, trying to hold on to at least a measure of calm.

Norris studied him. "You fellows had a bit of trouble last night, apparently. Care to tell me about it?"

Carefully the boy repeated the same story he had given to the other officers earlier in the day. The police chief listened without commenting.

When Bucky was through describing the getaway and the morning's arrest, the man reached into his pocket and pulled out a pair of glasses. Squinting as he examined the police report on his desk, he finally looked at Bucky.

"Well, son, you know how serious a thing like this could be. Running through traffic lights, evading lawful authority, charging through town at 80 miles an hour."

"Yes, sir."

"On the other hand, you say you weren't driving. Furthermore, you tried repeatedly to get Mr. Shultz to stop. Is that correct?"

A prayer in his heart, Bucky nodded.

The silver-haired law officer set down the report. "Just before I called you in here, I was on the phone with the police department down at Hampton Beach. Couple of the fellows there I know pretty well."

Bucky felt a sudden twinge of . . . of what?

"I'll tell you what they told me," the chief went on. "Apparently they know you from some experience you had down there at First California Bank about a year ago. A holdup and hostage situation. And then some business with basketball and point spreads."

The boy gulped. "Yes, sir."

"Anyway, they told me, 'If Mr. Stone says he wasn't driving, then he wasn't driving. Period, case closed.' Then they said this too: 'Mr. Stone has a pretty decent reputation in this town.' End of quote."

His heart pounding, Bucky flushed.

The officer stood up. "Mr. Stone, you and the young ladies are free to go. I'm sorry this has been such a difficult day for you."

The sense of relief felt like a warm bath flooding him. "Boy, I can't tell you . . . how much I appreciate this," he managed.

"Well, a good reputation can sometimes be worth more than, well, just about anything." For the first time Bucky saw a trace of a smile on the police chief's face.

Bucky took a deep breath. "What about Jonathan?"

The officer picked up the police report. "Well, we did get hold of his parents about half an hour ago," he said. "Mr. Shultz is driving up here this evening to help his son out. Of course, your friend will be facing some difficulty, as you can understand. License revoked, etc., etc. He won't be driving for quite some time."

"What do the rest of us do?" Bucky wanted to know.

Chief Norris came over and put a hand on his shoulder. "This is kind of unusual," he observed. "I'll tell what we'd really like for you to do."

"Sure."

"My advice is for you and the young ladies to just return right home. I don't know what kind of outing you were on, but your best bet is to head straight back to Hampton Beach right now. Take the van and go."

"But what about Jonathan?"

The officer nodded. "Like I said, his father's on his way. However things turn out, he can return home with him once bail's set and so forth. If it goes that far." He sat down next to the youth. "But really, for the sake of the proceedings here, I think it would be best for you to return to Hampton immediately and check in with the P.D. there before going home. I've already indicated to them that we'll try to have the three of you there by 10:00 this evening."

Bucky swallowed hard. "We're not still in . . . any kind of trouble, are we?"

"Oh, no," Chief Norris assured. "But we need to

follow a correct procedure here, and the three of you were technically involved in some very serious infractions. Until it all gets pleaded out, as we say, we need to have you follow the letter of the law. But with what your people down at Hampton have shared with me, I can promise you there's not going to be any problem."

Despite the overwhelming feeling of relief, an undefined sense of unfulfilled responsibility bothered Bucky. An image of Jonathan, seated alone in a bare holding room, tugged at him. "Do you mind if I ask you a question?"

"Not at all."

Bucky shifted in his seat. "I really don't feel very good about leaving Jonathan here by himself. I mean, I know he messed up and everything. But I'm still his friend. Wouldn't it be all right to wait here with him until his dad came?" The words ended on a hopeful note.

The police chief appeared nonplussed by the suggestion. "Do you mean it? You'd really stick around to help him out after all this?" He gave a little *humph*. "I mean, he was halfway willing to paste the whole thing on you. By not answering our questions. At least that's how I look at it."

With a wince Bucky realized that something inside him screamed to just get away from it all and head home with the girls. He fought back the temptation. "He's just scared," he murmured. "He panicked and just lost his head. But he's really not a bad guy."

"That may be." Chief Norris gave a little shrug.

"But this is still a pretty serious lineup of violations here. Evading lawful authority isn't ever taken lightly in this town." He drummed a pencil on his desk for a moment. "Well, Stone, from what the boys down at Hampton Beach told me, I should have expected something like this from you." After glancing down at a gold wristwatch, he said, "Mr. Shultz probably won't get in here until 7:00 or 8:00 tonight. That'd have you getting home at 3:00 or so in the morning. We can't do that."

"I really hate to leave him here all by himself," he repeated. "We could go home first thing in the morning."

After a moment of reflection, the officer nodded. "OK, Stone, if that's the way you want it. I'll call down there and tell them what's happening. I'll still want you to check in there as soon as you get in tomorrow afternoon. Just so things are by the book, like I said."

CHAPTER 13

JUST THE THREE OF US

Jonathan listened dully as Bucky explained to him all that had transpired. "So I'm a cooked goose, sounds like," he said without bitterness.

"It's not as bad as that," Bucky pointed out. "Your dad is on his way to help work it all out. And we're going to stay right here until he comes."

An unfamiliar though fleeting expression of gratitude crossed the older student's face. "I guess I ought to thank you," he muttered. "Instead of screaming at you for, you know, just telling the cops what happened."

"Aaaah, don't worry about it," Bucky asserted. "The girls and I will stay right here until your dad comes, and then head home tomorrow. And I guess you can ride back with your dad."

Jonathan nodded wearily. "Guess I won't be driving for a long time."

Bucky nodded. "Hey, I figure it's just a lesson all of us had to learn." He leaned closer to his friend. "I just feel bad that you're kind of the one who has to carry the bulk of it. I mean that."

Jonathan looked at his friend. "Sorry it turned out like this. I mean, missing the games and now sittin' here for hours and everything."

"Forget it," Bucky reminded him. "We're friends." He forced a grin. "It's still you and me against Tracy the Genius in chem lab."

The long April afternoon passed slowly. Tracy and Jill, informed of the outcome, stayed with the two boys for a while before deciding to hike over to a nearby mall to pass the time. Bucky called his father back to let him know what had happened, then, anxiously monitoring the contents of his wallet, brought some Del Taco food in for himself and Jonathan. They ate slowly, trying to make the time go by.

It was just past sundown when Mr. Shultz finally walked into the front door of the Eugene police station. A big man, he bore some resemblance to his stocky son as he looked around and finally spotted the four students.

He glanced briefly at the others before addressing Jonathan. "Guess you got in a fix, boy." His son nodded without speaking.

"So what's happening here?"

Officer Shelton, himself showing signs of weariness after a long Friday in uniform, walked over and explained the situation. "Bucky, here, and the girls, wanted to stay with Jonathan until you arrived. They'll be heading home first thing in the morning, I guess."

"What about us?" Mr. Shultz appeared to be unmoved by the fact that his son's friends had remained with Jonathan.

"Well, we're willing to release Jonathan into your supervision," the officer observed. "We do have traffic court on Saturdays, but it runs just from ten to noon, so we'll need for both of you to be here for that."

"That's it?"

"For now, I think so." The policeman turned to Bucky and the two girls. "The three of you are all set? You know about checking in down at Hampton when you get home?"

Bucky nodded.

"OK, then. You kids can head out. We have just a little bit of paperwork to do here with Mr. Shultz." He looked at Bucky a moment, then said softly, "You did your friend a real favor by staying."

With Jonathan's keys in his pocket, Bucky went over and shook goodbye with him. "Hang in there, man. I'll be praying for you."

Fatigue in his eyes, the boy nodded. "Thanks, Stone. You really . . ." He didn't finish the sentence.

With Tracy in the passenger seat, Bucky carefully drove the maroon van over to the same motel where they had spent the previous evening. Again borrowing cash from the two girls, he paid for two rooms and sank down into the quiet solitude of his own bed with a sigh of weary relief.

The evening shadows casting the room in a murky darkness reminded him that it was now Sabbath. He thought of Mom and Rachel Marie back in Hampton Beach and their pleasant Friday evening worships by the fireplace with religious music on their CD player.

There was a knock on the door. "Yeah, come in." He stirred on the bed.

Tracy and Jill entered with a big carton in their hands. "Pizza girls," Tracy announced with a giggle.

"Are you kidding?" Bucky had almost forgotten how hungry he was. The aroma from the box was overpowering.

"Somebody has to look after our knight in shining armor," Tracy grinned. She plopped down on the bed next to him. "Cheese, tomato, olives—the works."

He shot her a grateful grin as he pulled a piece free and took a big bite. "Man, this is gonna save my life."

"Well, we figured after the kind of day we had, we deserved a treat," Jill added, taking a nibble of her own slice.

The next half hour was a welcome change from the previous 30 hours as they ate and talked. Both girls had a thoughtful side, Bucky noticed, as they spoke sympathetically about Jonathan's dilemma.

It was Jill who finally stretched and yawned. "I'm pooped, you guys."

"Yeah." Bucky picked up the pizza wrappings and stuffed them into the motel room's trash can. "Plus we got a long drive home tomorrow."

The dark-haired girl climbed to her feet. "Come on, Tracy. Let's go to bed."

Tracy, still reclining on the guest bed with a nearly

empty cup of Pepsi, didn't move. "Go ahead," she said. "I'll be over in a little bit."

Jill glanced over at Bucky with a grin. "Well, OK." She opened the door while fumbling in the pocket to her jeans. "I guess I have the key. Boy, it's nice out here."

The redhead, wearing a little strawberry-red T-shirt and white shorts, looked over at Bucky. "Just you and two Hampton Beach beauty queens," she grinned.

"Yeah." He shifted nervously from his perch on the other bed. The girl's presence in his motel room gave him an odd tingle. "You want to . . . go for a walk or anything?"

"I don't feel like it," she murmured, looking up at him.

"I know, but . . ." His voice suddenly felt awkward. "Maybe we should anyway."

"How come?" She gave him a quizzical look.

Bucky looked directly at her, trying to think of a reasonable answer. "I just . . . well, it's only you and me in here."

"I won't attack you."

"I know." He climbed to his feet. "But it doesn't look right."

"Oh, who cares?" She stayed right where she was.

Picking up the motel room key, he sat back down on the chair next to the bed where Tracy was reclining. "I guess I care what people think of you," he said at last. "And I care what I think of you."

She gave him a little smile that brought dimples to her cheeks. "What *do* you think of me?" Her eyes had an expectant sparkle to them.

As he answered he pulled on a jacket. "Come on for a walk, and I'll tell you." He forced a grin.

Outside the Oregon air was comfortably cool as they walked down the quiet street. Tracy, her hands thrust into her jacket pockets, said nothing for nearly a block.

It was Bucky who broke the silence. Fumbling at first, but with a growing confidence, he told her of his decision the night before. "Being a Christian is the number one thing in my life," he said, looking directly at her. "And I've already found out the hard way that for me to go out with someone who isn't interested in it too . . . just doesn't work at all. It ends up not being fair to her." There. It was out.

She seemed to accept his explanation. "But who said I wasn't interested in it?" she put in.

"Are you?"

A pause. "Not really. At least I've never been before."

Bucky didn't say anything. The silence between them was not uncomfortable. He sensed that she had already suspected his faith might be a difficulty.

Quietly they walked back to the motel. Despite the upheaval of the aborted trip, Bucky felt a quiet sense of peace. In finding the strength to openly speak about his faith to Tracy, had he turned some kind of corner?

They arrived back at the girls' room. "I guess I'll see you both in the morning," Bucky said.

She looked up at him, trying not to smile as they both became aware of the 17-inch height gap between them. "See, it would never have worked anyway," he said softly.

For a moment Tracy didn't answer as she gazed into his eyes. Then without warning she reached up and tugged on his shoulder. Without meaning to, he bent over just a bit. Standing on her tiptoes, she gave him a kiss that lingered for several seconds.

"Think about that," she murmured, turning away and slipping the key into the knob of her room. And then she was gone.

CHAPTER 14

ENDINGS AND BEGINNINGS

Bucky was just climbing into bed when he realized he hadn't called Lisa back. Trying not to think about Tracy's kiss, he picked up the phone and dialed the familiar number up in Seattle.

The sound of a man's voice on the other end made Bucky start. "This is Bucky Stone. Is Lisa there?"

Her father did not say anything. It was nearly a minute before Lisa came on the line. "Hi."

"How are you doing?"

"OK." She gave a nervous little laugh. "Are you in the state pen or what?"

He explained what had happened and apologized for the trip being cut short. "I really wish I could see you," he confessed, "but they want us to head right home and check in down there."

Lisa sighed. "I kind of figured things were going to

get all screwed up," she admitted, a trace of frustration in her voice. "But I guess we should be glad you're not in any kind of trouble."

"Well, listen," he responded. "I know you're weary of hearing it, but I really am going to get up there to see you. Soon, I mean."

"I'll be waiting right here."

Bucky drifted off to sleep thinking to himself that, despite all that had happened, there was still something very special about Lisa.

The next morning it was a sober trio that pulled out of the motel's small parking lot in the Chevy van. Even though Bucky had never really discussed the Sabbath with Tracy and Jill, both of the girls somehow sensed that it was a different kind of day. The hours rolled by quietly on I-5 without the usual wails of heavy rock music.

"Sorry you missed all those A's games," Tracy said softly to him as they stopped for a gasoline fill-up.

He nodded, pushing aside the unhappy sensation that came from purchasing gas on the Sabbath. "No big deal. There's plenty of baseball back home." He thought for a moment about the Panthers' frosh team and the remaining schedule of games with Dan.

"Do you miss being on varsity?"

"Sure." He turned on the van's big engine and pulled onto the freeway again. "But it's worth it."

Tracy's eyes were thoughtful as she looked over at him. In the back, Jill, who had the entire seat to herself, was engrossed in a novel.

"I thought a lot about, you know, last night."

Bucky couldn't help but smile. "Yeah. Me too."

She ran her fingers through her curly hair. "You mind if I ask you something?"

"What?"

For a moment the redhead seemed almost unsure of herself. "Well, it's just . . . you're probably the nicest guy I know at school. I mean, with this cop business and everything. I don't know of anybody else who has the . . ." She tried to think of the right word. "Integrity, I guess. You just have a lot of class. Staying up there to help Jonathan out and all that."

His heart did a little flip-flip, but he managed to force a smile. "Hey, please go on. Tell me more."

The girl looked directly at him. "Well, on the one hand you're a great guy. And on the other hand, you're a . . . born-again type. And I guess I just don't know how to put it all together." Tracy paused. "And how to get what I want." She said the last without blushing.

As he hesitated, he had for really the first time in his life a sense of discussing important issues with another person his age. He looked over at her.

"I guess it's possible," he said slowly, "for someone to be nice . . . and kind and honest and all that—without being a Christian. But for me the two go together. It's being a Christian—Christ *in me*—that makes me what I am." He changed lanes before looking over at her again. "Whether that's good or not, I guess is up to somebody like you."

"But how does it *work*?" She leaned closer to him, her slim body restrained by the seatbelt. "I don't know of anybody except for you who really has being a Christian work for them."

A road sign flashed by: "Welcome to California!" He pointed at it with a grin before answering. "I guess you just decide that God and Jesus come before everything else," he explained. "At least in our Adventist Church, that's what we hang onto. You follow Jesus wherever He leads. In your friendships, in how you live and treat people—everything."

The miles rolled by as the conversation continued. Tracy, despite her sometimes flippant personality, had a deep spiritual hunger that showed in the thoughtful questions she raised. At one point he threw up both hands with a laugh, pretending to let the van swerve for just a moment.

"Boy, when somebody as smart as you gets around to asking the right questions, I have to run and get my Bible." He gave her an approving grin, trying in vain to cope with the growing affection he felt for her.

It was late afternoon before they pulled up at the familiar police department in Hampton Beach. Several officers Bucky recognized from last semester's point-shaving scam gathered around to hear about the episode in Eugene. A scant 20 minutes after arriving, Bucky and the girls wheeled out and headed for Jill's home.

"I guess I'll see you in school Monday," he told Tracy as he helped carry her tote bag to the Givenchys' front door.

"I keep feeling like this is Sunday already," she said with a little pout.

"Yeah, me too." Several times that afternoon he'd been forced to remind himself that it was Sabbath.

At the front door they paused. "Bucky, I . . ."
Again the redhead had a momentary lapse in poise.
"It's been interesting." A laugh. "I guess that's what
they always say after an adventure."

He nodded.

"I can't think of anybody else I could have talked
about things like this with," she added, putting a hand
on his arm. "Thanks."

Bucky got home just in time for sundown worship.
"Boy, I'm glad I don't have Sabbaths like this one very
often," he murmured as he sprawled by the familiar
fireplace in the living room.

His mother reached over and gave his hair an
affectionate mussing. "I'm glad you're home, honey."

* * *

The remaining weeks of school fell into place in
rapid succession. Jonathan, back to school for Monday's chem lab, reluctantly shared the news that his
license had been suspended for three years. "Plus
$400," he grumbled.

"Man, that's too bad," Bucky commiserated,
thinking to himself that it could certainly have been
worse. Tracy, her perky self again, took charge of the
day's assigned experiment. For the moment the
romantic mood of the past weekend seemed to be
little more than a pleasant memory.

The Litton/Stone hitting parade picked up right
where it left off as the two star athletes powered the
Panther frosh team to five wins in a row before their
first defeat. The squad ended the school year with a
record of 13 and 3, much to Coach Walker's delight.

"What I wouldn't have given to have the two of

you over on varsity, though," he grumbled good-naturedly after the final contest, a classic come-from-behind win for the Hampton team. The varsity Panthers had gone into an extended slump the last two weeks and had missed the playoff round entirely.

"Maybe next year," Bucky suggested, always the optimist. "Get us a schedule with no Friday nights on it."

Graduation night was an electrifying event. Despite his earlier vows, Bucky felt a stir of excitement when Tracy sat down beside him and Dan as Sam and the other seniors paraded in to the slow strains of "Pomp and Circumstance." It was the only traditional element of the evening, as endless catcalls, sirens, and confetti interrupted the procedures. Even Bucky got caught up in it.

The biggest surprise of the evening came when the name "Sam Trung Minh" was announced with the second highest cumulative GPA among the senior class. "Man, I didn't know he was up there that high!" Bucky said to Dan. He leaned over toward Tracy. "He's almost as smart as you are." She laughed, her red curls shaking.

At the back of the huge athletic field, Pastor Jensen gave the boys an enthusiastic greeting. "Good show!" he grinned as he examined Sam's Merit Certificate. "I had no idea you were pulling in so many A's. I should have you write my sermons for me." He greeted the senior's Vietnamese parents warmly.

"Honey, we'll see you back at the house," Mom said as she took Dad's hand. "Come on, Rachel Marie." She waved to Sam again. "Congratulations."

"Thanks for the present," the tall senior said, setting the package on top of a pile of gifts.

A few seconds later, Bucky found an opportunity to introduce Tracy to the pastor. "Well, good evening, young lady," Jensen said with a big smile. "One more year, and you folks will be doing all the celebrating."

"Yeah, she'll be sitting up there in the valedictorian's chair," Bucky reminded.

Pastor Jensen glanced around at the thinning crowds as if to look for somebody. "You fellows be sure to get to church on time Sabbath," he advised. "I've got a big surprise for you."

One of the seniors from the varsity basketball team came ambling by with his arm around his girlfriend. "Hey, Stone!" He accepted a high five of congratulations. "We're having a party over at my place. Got about a hundred bucks' worth of pizza waiting for us and everything." Then he caught himself with a grin. "You know, just soda and stuff. It's cool." Glancing over at Tracy, he added, "You too, Tracy. You can do some physics problems for us if we run out of videos." Looking at both Dan and Bucky, he asked, "What do you say?"

Bucky hesitated as he glanced over at Tracy. In a new dress and with her cheeks still flushed with the excitement of graduation, she had never looked prettier. A party? Something inside him threatened to pull itself loose.

Then he took a deep breath. "I . . . I guess I better not," he said at last. "Sorry."

The senior looked confused as he glanced over at Tracy. She shook her head too. At last he shrugged.